S0-CBT-610

"Are you pregnant?"

Soleil felt a pinch of conscience at West's question. Accidentally running into each other was *not* how she'd hoped to tell him the news.

She plastered on a smile. "Yes, I am! Isn't it great?"

"Wow," he said, looking bewildered. "Who… uh, who's your partner?"

Okay, so maybe he hadn't done the math. Maybe *I'm having your kid* wasn't tattooed on her forehead.

"Actually," she said, stalling for time and hating herself for it, "the father isn't in the picture."

This was the line she'd been giving everyone who asked. Only, it wasn't true anymore. Not exactly.

Because he was most definitely in the picture again.

And she had a lot of explaining to do.

Dear Reader,

I grew up in a house full of Harlequin romance novels. My mother was an avid reader, and as soon as I was old enough to be curious about the books that filled her shelves, I became a fan of the genre myself. Stories about strong women and dashing men had endless appeal for me. I even tried my hand writing a romance story in middle school, much to the chagrin of my English teacher. Still, I had some growing up to do before I would understand much about the complications of falling in love.

After graduating from college, armed with a bit more information about the ways of the world, I decided to give romance writing another try. Five years later, I was thrilled to sell my first novel to Harlequin. Seeing my book in print with the company that had spawned my love for the genre felt like coming full circle, and to this day, I'm still proud to write for a publisher that celebrates the hopes and fantasies of women around the world.

I love to hear from readers. You can reach me and find out about my upcoming releases at my Web site, www.jamiesobrato.com.

Sincerely,

Jamie Sobrato

Baby Under the Mistletoe
Jamie Sobrato

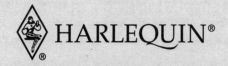

TORONTO • NEW YORK • LONDON
AMSTERDAM • PARIS • SYDNEY • HAMBURG
STOCKHOLM • ATHENS • TOKYO • MILAN • MADRID
PRAGUE • WARSAW • BUDAPEST • AUCKLAND

If you purchased this book without a cover you should be aware that this book is stolen property. It was reported as "unsold and destroyed" to the publisher, and neither the author nor the publisher has received any payment for this "stripped book."

Recycling programs
for this product may
not exist in your area.

ISBN-13: 978-0-373-71604-3

BABY UNDER THE MISTLETOE

Copyright © 2009 by Jamie Sobrato.

All rights reserved. Except for use in any review, the reproduction or utilization of this work in whole or in part in any form by any electronic, mechanical or other means, now known or hereafter invented, including xerography, photocopying and recording, or in any information storage or retrieval system, is forbidden without the written permission of the publisher, Harlequin Enterprises Limited, 225 Duncan Mill Road, Don Mills, Ontario, Canada M3B 3K9.

This is a work of fiction. Names, characters, places and incidents are either the product of the author's imagination or are used fictitiously, and any resemblance to actual persons, living or dead, business establishments, events or locales is entirely coincidental.

This edition published by arrangement with Harlequin Books S.A.

® and TM are trademarks of the publisher. Trademarks indicated with ® are registered in the United States Patent and Trademark Office, the Canadian Trade Marks Office and in other countries.

www.eHarlequin.com

Printed in U.S.A.

ABOUT THE AUTHOR

Jamie Sobrato has written nineteen novels for Harlequin. She spent her earliest years on a farm in rural Kentucky, before moving across the country and around the world. Upon seeing the majestic redwoods and rugged beaches of Northern California, she knew she'd found her permanent home, where she now lives with her two children. Jamie can be reached through her Web site, www.jamiesobrato.com.

Books by Jamie Sobrato

HARLEQUIN SUPERROMANCE
1536—A FOREVER FAMILY

HARLEQUIN BLAZE
237—ONCE UPON A SEDUCTION
266—THE SEX QUOTIENT
284—A WHISPER OF WANTING
316—SEX AS A SECOND LANGUAGE
328—CALL ME WICKED
357—SEX BOMB
420—SEDUCING A S.E.A.L.
490—MADE YOU LOOK

Don't miss any of our special offers. Write to us at the following address for information on our newest releases.

Harlequin Reader Service
U.S.: 3010 Walden Ave., P.O. Box 1325, Buffalo, NY 14269
Canadian: P.O. Box 609, Fort Erie, Ont. L2A 5X3

To my grandmother, Mary Gentry,
who helped shape my earliest memories of
good food and farm life.

I love you, Granny.

PROLOGUE

HE WAS ALL WRONG for her.

Everything from the color of his skin to the jagged scar across his forearm, the result of some unsavory Special Forces operation, indicated that they were two different people from two incongruent worlds.

Which was what made West Morgan the perfect summer distraction. He'd be gone tomorrow, and Soleil Freeman would never miss him.

Okay, she would miss *this,* but not *him.*

This, as in the adult conversation, the grown-up closeness. It was something she rarely had in her everyday life, with a houseful of teenagers for whom she played mentor, coach, social worker and teacher. Those kids were her life, but with their endless needs and sad personal histories, they could suck the life right out of her if she wasn't careful.

So for a few weeks, spending her free time with someone unsuitable was exactly what she needed to put everything back in balance.

Soleil's hand dangled over the edge of the canoe, trailing through the icy water of Promise Lake. From beneath the wide brim of a straw hat, she watched West's dark head bent over her, kissing the flat of her belly. His lips, a mere butterfly flutter, sent shivers through her in spite of the warm day.

When he spotted her gooseflesh, he looked up and smiled. His face was so arresting, it never failed to give her a little thrill. Icy blue eyes, a full, sensual mouth and dark hair a little longer than the military regulations allowed. Special Forces could get away with the longer hair, he claimed. They had to blend in, look like civilians.

She didn't know if he was telling the truth, and she didn't really care. He was gorgeous, a lovely distraction, though not the kind of guy she normally went for. He didn't own a single item of hemp clothing, couldn't carry on a conversation about French poets to save his life and wouldn't have been caught dead driving around in a car festooned with Save the Endangered Condor bumper stickers. In short, he was nowhere near in danger of worming his way into her heart. Couldn't even see her heart from where he stood.

Soleil wore a black bikini, and he, a pair of navy swim trunks, but they hadn't dared swim yet in the cold water. Instead, they'd paddled to the middle of the lake to have a picnic lunch and now were simply floating there, soaking up the sun.

A speculative expression crossed his face. "Do you ever think about having a family?" he asked, a question so out of the blue Soleil laughed in surprise.

But he was serious.

"Why do you ask?"

"Just curious."

"When you look at me, do you see a baby-making machine?"

He flashed a sly grin. "Yep."

"If that's your idea of smooth talk, I can see why you're thirty-seven and still single."

"Maybe I'm still single because I've never met a woman I'd want to make a baby with. Maybe you're the first one."

Nausea struck her. Until this moment, they'd seemed equally intent on keeping things casual.

"I don't want kids," she said.

She loved children, but there was no way she could have one of her own and continue to do the work she did. And that work was too important to the future communities of the kids she mentored to abandon.

Besides, after surviving her own hippiefied Berkeley childhood, she was hardly a candidate for the home-baked-cookies-and-suburban-play-groups crowd. Even with their limited time together, Soleil knew beyond a doubt that picket fences and minivans featured large in West's ideal future.

"Oh, come on. Every woman wants to settle down and pop out a few kids."

"*Every* woman? Did you grow up in a fifties sit-com or something?"

He smirked. He was pushing her buttons because

he enjoyed her temper. And even though she recognized that he was playing again with her, she couldn't avoid reacting. She was furious.

"You'd look hot in an apron, barefoot and pregnant—"

"Shut up," she said through clenched teeth.

"It would be great. You could be at home all day with the kids, taking care of the house."

One more word, and—

"You could be my little woman, and I could be your—"

Fury like a white-hot rod of lightning shot through her. She thrust all her weight into his chest, knocking him backward. He lost his balance and went over the side of the boat, into the lake. She caught the surprise on his face just before he hit the water and enjoyed a moment of satisfaction as she steadied herself against the rocking. Then she grabbed a paddle with shaking hands, not bothering to look back as she propelled the canoe toward the dock.

"Hey!" he called out, but she kept going. They hadn't gone out so far that he couldn't swim to shore. He was a strong swimmer, after all.

Eventually, she cast a glance over her shoulder to make sure he was okay, and his steady freestyle stroke assured her he was fine.

Unlike her. She was still shaking with anger. Or was it fear?

Fear, yes, maybe. Because it wasn't West she was paddling away from so much as the suffocating idea of the future he painted.

It wasn't *her* future, not by a long shot.

CHAPTER ONE

SOLEIL FREEMAN was pregnant.

Knocked up, preggo, with child, carrying a bun in the oven, in the family way, et cetera.

Five and a half months so, to be exact.

Even if this fact had not permeated every moment of every day of her waking consciousness, she would still have known it by the uncomfortable thickness in her middle and the constant, burning desire she had to eat everything in sight.

To say this *development* wasn't in her plans was an understatement. For a variety of reasons—some of which would require the professional supervision of a therapist to sort out—Soleil hadn't factored kids into her life. Certainly not single parenthood and certainly not now when running her youth program on her organic farm took every ounce of her energy. How she would even manage a baby in the mix baffled her. Especially on days like today.

It was a damp gray morning on Rainbow Farm, and Soleil was not in the mood to search for a lost goat. A lost cheeseburger, maybe, but missing livestock? This was only going to postpone lunch—provided the animal was found quickly and safely.

If not… She hurried across the front lawn, feeling about as lithe and agile as a watermelon. She'd once been a track star in high school and later at U.C. Berkeley. She'd been able to sprint so fast, she'd felt at certain blissful moments as if the wind carried her.

But now? She could still run, but the pace had no familiarity with wind-assisted agility, and her litheness was tempered by a paranoia that with every step she was going to inadvertently cause herself to miscarry. The doctor had assured her that wasn't going to happen, that she could still run as long as she felt good doing so, but pregnancy was doing crazy things to her brain. She was hyperaware that another being's life depended on her completely. Frankly, the pressure was getting to her.

Behind Soleil, Malcolm, one of her current interns from Oakland, plodded along, apparently not wanting to seem as if he cared about anything in the world. It wasn't cool to hurry, and especially not for a lost goat.

"How did the goat get away from you?" she called over her shoulder.

"How should I know?" came Malcolm's surly answer.

"Where's Silas?"

Silas was her cattle dog, a mostly Australian shepherd fully capable of managing a herd of goats on his own without any help from the teens.

"Tonio's afraid of dogs."

Right. She'd confined Silas to the barn due to the boy's sheer terror at the sight of him. But she'd probably find the missing goat a lot faster with the dog's help.

"Tell Tonio to go inside so I can let the dog out, okay?"

"Okay," Malcolm said, and sauntered toward the field, clearly happy to get out of the goat-searching mission.

She went into the barn and called for the dog, then told him to find the lost goat. He didn't need any further coaxing. He simply watched her face as she talked, with his eerily smart blue eyes, then took off at a full run.

Following, Soleil passed the garden, where two of the teenagers, Lexie and Angelique, were picking squash for tonight's dinner. Both still unaccustomed to getting their hands dirty, they were handling the vegetables as if the plants might jump out and bite them, which begged the question of why they'd applied for internships, but Soleil knew better than to expect to turn a bunch of city kids into earth mothers in such a short time.

She arrived at the field where she could see one boy, Jordan, overseeing the nine goats who hadn't run off. This field bordered one of the main roads into town, and there was a section of fence that needed repairing, which meant there was a chance the errant goat could make it to the road and get hit. With that thought, she quickened her pace up the hill. At the top stood a grove of oak and bay trees, and beyond them was the road where she could barely hear the sound of passing cars.

Halfway up the hill, she heard Silas's bark indicating he'd located the goat. But a second distressed bark told her something was wrong.

She scrambled the rest of the way up, then through the grove of trees. There she saw the source of the trouble—the goat on the far side of the road. Silas paced before her in a panic because he knew better than to cross the dangerous roadway.

The goat, for its part, didn't know any better. And before Soleil could do anything, the goat took a few tentative steps into the road just as a car rounded the bend fifty feet away. The driver, in a black SUV, slammed on the brakes, swerving into the next lane.

Soleil could only cover her face and pray as she heard the car skidding to a stop.

A moment passed, silent, without any sickening thud of bumper against flesh, and she opened her eyes to see the car stopped a foot away from the goat, who was staring at it nonplussed.

"Jules!" she called to the goat, whom she could identify now by the animal's white markings. "Get over here now!"

The dog barked again, but she commanded him to

stay as she looked both ways before crossing. She walked to retrieve the immobile goat.

Only then did she take a close look at the driver of the SUV and notice that he seemed to be taking a close look at her.

Because they knew each other.

Dark brown, wavy hair, blue eyes she'd spent more than a few lazy summer afternoons gazing into, a mouth that could make a girl entertain naughty thoughts….

"West Morgan?" she said stupidly, as if he could hear her from inside the car.

But he could, because he'd just rolled down his window.

West. The one man she desperately wanted to avoid right now.

"Wily goat, eh?"

"I'm so sorry!" she said. "Thank goodness you weren't hurt."

Soleil grabbed the goat by the scruff and gave her a good shove with her thigh to get Jules moving in the right direction.

Hustle now. No need to linger in the middle of the road with West Morgan waiting.

She hoped like crazy he'd drive off now that the road was clear, Instead, he pulled to the shoulder.

Dammit. Dammit, dammit, dammit.

She sucked in her belly and tried her best not to look pregnant.

But everyone who'd seen her lately knew she'd

gained a lot of weight on her formerly thin frame. Even if West couldn't see her belly beneath the baggy wool sweater and corduroy jacket she was wearing, he could surely see the ever-widening thighs encased in jeans that used to be too big, and the meat-loaf-enhanced chipmunk cheeks she'd grown since their last encounter.

"Hey," he said once he'd gotten out of the car and propped his elbows on the roof. "Need any help goatherding?"

"No, thanks!" she said too cheerily.

She nodded to Silas, and the dog gave the goat a commanding bark, then lightly nipped its haunch. That was all the encouragement Jules needed to amble through the fence in the direction of the field.

West, ignoring her desperate vibes telling him to get lost, glanced in both directions, waited for a truck to pass, then crossed the road.

He extended his arms once he was within a few feet of her, giving her no escape from full-body contact. Soleil gave him an awkward hug, trying not to let him feel the hard little basketball that was her stomach.

She failed.

"Whoa," he said when her belly bumped against him. He pulled back and looked down.

Up close, there was no way not to notice, with her short torso that left no extra room for a fetus to spread out and relax, that she was pregnant.

"Are you—"

His question hung half formed in the air as he seemed to realize simultaneously that "Are you pregnant?" was one of the dumbest questions anyone could ask a woman, and if she was, then the fact that they'd been lovers this past summer might make the news relevant for him.

This was *not* how she'd hoped he'd find out.

He seemed to gather his thoughts as he said again, "Are you pregnant?"

Soleil plastered on a smile. "Yes, I am! Isn't it great?"

"Wow," he said, looking bewildered. "Who…"

He went pale.

Okay, so maybe he hadn't done the math after all. There was a much bigger discussion to be had between them, but it wasn't one she wanted to have at the side of the road where her interns could interrupt. She had a schedule to keep, lunch to prepare. Lord, she was hungry.

"Actually," she said, stalling for time. "The father isn't in the picture."

This was the line she'd been giving everyone who asked.

Only, it wasn't true anymore. Not exactly.

Because he was in the picture again. He'd almost run over her goat.

And he deserved a better explanation than she'd just given him.

WEST MORGAN HAD BEEN so preoccupied on the drive back to Promise, he almost hadn't seen the goat standing in the middle of the road. Thank God for antilock brakes.

And even now, his brain was a muddle of conflicting thoughts as he tried to make sense of the fact that Soleil Freeman, the woman he'd spent the past five and a half months trying to forget, was standing in front of him, pregnant.

What the hell?

Still beautiful, perhaps even more so now, her formerly wiry frame had been softened by lush curves. She'd done something with her hair, too. In the summer it had been a wild mess of springy curls, but she had it in two braids today that gave her a young earth-goddess aura.

He stared into her pale green eyes, made all the more stunning by her café-au-lait skin, trying to see some truth there that hadn't been spoken aloud yet.

But all he saw was her looking as though she wanted to get away from him. The thin, brittle smile she wore wasn't fooling anyone, definitely not him.

"Um, I would stay and catch up," Soleil said after an awkward silence, "but I've left the kids unsupervised on the farm and I need to get back there. I'm shorthanded today."

She was already edging toward her property, stepping over a downed section of fencing.

"Hey, can I help you out? My dad isn't expecting

me for a few more hours." West had the feeling Soleil would disappear forever if he didn't pin her down right now. Ridiculous thought, given how tied she was to the farm. Still, he couldn't let this conversation end with so many questions forming in his head.

"Oh. No, thank you, but no. Really, I'll be fine."

"Looks like you need a fence repair."

She glanced down. "Right. Before any more goats escape. Thanks for the reminder—I'll get someone on it."

"Seriously, I'd love to see what you've got going on around here. Why don't you let me stick around for a while, do a quick fix on the fence and give you a hand wherever else you need it. In fact, I insist."

Soleil looked like a cornered animal. Her eyes wide, she froze—probably contemplating her options.

Before she could produce an argument, he closed the deal, "I'll drive around to the house and come find you once I've parked."

"Oh. Well," she said as he crossed the road to his SUV. "Really, I don't need your help."

But she did. She was meticulous enough that she'd never let a section of fence remain unmended unless she was overwhelmed.

On the short trip to the farmhouse, his brain tried to make sense of Soleil being pregnant, while doing the math. Even without knowing how far along she was, there was every reason to believe he was responsible.

Yet her comment about the father not being in the picture implied that not only did the father know about the kid, but also that he'd chosen not to participate. That ruled West out, didn't it? No way would he bow out of his kid's life. Especially if Soleil was the mother. Men looked their whole lives for a woman as sexy, smart, beautiful, funny and capable as Soleil.

Besides, they'd taken precautions against this very thing happening. They'd used a condom—every time.

Wait. There had been that one time when the condom supply had run out. They'd both sworn to being healthy and she'd claimed to be on the pill. Hadn't she? Or had he filled in the blank in his urgency to get her naked? Either way, did it really matter? If he was the father, wasn't figuring out the details of when and who said what akin to closing the barn door after the horse escaped—or, more appropriately, fixing the fence after the goat got out?

The more important aspect was what to do from here. And that necessitated talking to Soleil—openly and honestly. Something he didn't hold out a lot of hope for if her earlier evasion was anything to go by.

But maybe there was a reason for that evasiveness. Maybe he was jumping to conclusions without all the facts. What if he wasn't the father? What if the father actually did know and chose not to be involved? What if the guy had dumped her and she was embarrassed about the situation? It seemed unlikely that Soleil would be dumped—it was far more probable

that *she'd* dumped *him.* That was her usual M.O.—
get out before emotions get too complicated.

Still, when would she have gotten pregnant by
someone else? Before West? After? The last time
they'd slept together had been in June, which would
make her five or so months pregnant now. He was no
expert on how big women got in any given month of
pregnancy, but she did look as if she was at least five
months along—not huge yet, but with a noticeable
bump in front. Was it possible there'd been someone
before or after him?

Dammit, he needed some clarification.

West parked in front of the white Victorian farmhouse, got out of the car and strode toward the field
behind the barn, his dread growing with each step. His
legs felt shaky, as if at any moment they might fail him.

Him, a father.

He couldn't be a father right now, could he? He'd
envisioned fatherhood occurring at some point off in
the distant and fuzzy future once he'd found someone
he liked enough to marry and settle down with. In the
meantime, he was too busy living life to worry about
the future.

But now…Soleil was pregnant.

Could he handle it? Did he have any choice?

He'd been in some pretty sketchy situations as a
Special Forces officer, but this notion of impending,
unexpected fatherhood—he'd never felt so terrified
in his life as he did right now.

CHAPTER TWO

SOLEIL NEEDED WEST showing up right now about as much as she needed a few more holes in the fence. Not only did she have to keep up her five teenage interns—without the help of her assistant, Michelle, who was out with the flu—but she had to act as their counselor, friend, warden and supervisor all day, too. She didn't have time for a major life drama on top of everything else.

She hadn't physically recovered from bumping into West. She was shaky still, and desperately wanted to hide out here in the barn with a box of Twinkies and a glass of milk until he went away.

But gastro-self-indulgence would have to wait. Right now she had to negotiate Silas and a teen terrified of all dogs.

"The dog won't hurt you, I promise." She reached for a dose of patience that seemed in short supply at the moment.

Tonio stood on the far side of the fence, refusing to enter the field and help with the goats so long as Silas was there.

"I already told you, I hate dogs." He eyed Silas and shook his head. "No way you're changing my mind."

She didn't want to deal with this. Not now, not with West lurking nearby, threatening to upset the balance of her universe.

"I understand how you feel. Dogs can be dangerous. Did you have a bad experience with one?"

He kept watching the dog as he answered. "Something like that."

"Why don't you tell me about it."

He shook his head.

"Here's my problem," Soleil said. "Silas is a working dog. He has an important job here at the farm, and if I keep him penned up in the barn, he can't do the work I need him to do, and more goats could wander off."

"I'm not helping with the goats then."

"Fair enough. For now, I'll find other work for you to do."

She didn't add that later, she'd get to the bottom of his dog fear, but she intended to. It was hard to go through life terrified of dogs, especially when that very fear could put Tonio in danger around aggressive canines. She took note of the pale, barely visible scars on his arms and neck and realized he'd likely been mauled.

A moment later, West appeared, striding toward them in that confident, ready-to-conquer-the-world way he had, and her hunger pangs morphed to anxiety.

She wasn't ready for him. Wasn't ready for this conversation. She'd known it was coming, but she'd thought she had more time. She'd expected him to show up in town for the holidays, and she'd planned to approach him in her own time, prepared to give him a firm talk about how she intended to raise the child on her own, and how he could have as much or as little involvement in the child's life as he wanted, but that she didn't need his help.

It all sounded so perfectly reasonable in her head, and yet, she was terrified of saying any of it aloud.

"Oh, hey," Soleil said stupidly. "You're here."

To Tonio, she said, "You've got chicken duty. You won't have to worry about the dog if you're in the chicken zone."

The chickens would keep him busy for a little while. They needed to be fed, and their coop cleaned once any fresh eggs had been collected. He'd already done the job twice thanks to his dog fear, so he knew the drill.

His shoulders slumped. "Do I have to? The chicken coop smells."

"Your other choice is mucking out the barn. Which would you like?"

"Chicken duty," he said sullenly, then slunk away.

West watched the boy go. "How's your current batch of kids doing?"

He'd spent enough time at the farm with her during the summer to have a rough idea what she did here—take the most promising applicants who applied to her program and give them an internship at the farm, where they could learn skills to take back to their community and help run urban-garden projects.

"They're doing well," she said, glad to focus on something innocuous.

He nodded. "I'm going to repair that fence. Where can I find a hammer and nails around here?"

She thought of protesting his help again, but really, she needed the fence fixed, and there wasn't much sense in turning down a free hand today. And if he was occupied away at the property line, she'd have time to mentally brace herself for the inevitable baby conversation.

"Just inside the barn, to the left, you'll find what you need."

He nodded, and strode toward the barn without another word. Something about his expression had been a little off. He hadn't looked as happy and relaxed as he had during their initial encounter.

Had he figured out the truth on his own? Well, duh. How could he not have?

She chewed the inside of her cheek, a nervous habit since childhood, and headed for the house to prepare lunch.

As she approached the porch, which was bedecked in wreaths and holiday garland she and the kids had hung the day before, it hit her that her own child would be playing here in a few years, toddling around after the ducks, swinging on the porch swing, pulling up flowers from the garden.

She may not be able to give her baby a perfect, intact nuclear family, but she could give the child this place—the happiest moments of her own childhood had happened here at this farm, and the same would be true for her baby. This idea, she loved.

Her own child.

The notion still made her a little dizzy sometimes. But she'd already felt the baby's fluttering first movements, had seen its tiny heart beating on an ultrasound screen, and she knew that soon enough, her reality would be permanently, drastically altered.

How would she do it? She didn't exactly have any great role models for motherhood to turn to. Her own mother's drinking, raging, depressive style was not one she would ever emulate. Or at least she hoped she wouldn't. With every ounce of her being she wanted to be a better mother than her own had been—more loving, more attentive, more centered.

And yet she didn't know how she'd do it.

Her train of thought was interrupted by a scream from inside the house, then someone else yelling, "Bitch!"

Soleil headed down the hall to the kitchen, where she found Lexie with milk dripping down the front of her, and Angelique looking as though she wanted to throttle her.

"What's going on here?" Soleil demanded.

"She called me a crack whore."

"You *are* one!" Lexie cried.

"Both of you, stop! Lexie, you go to the bathroom right now and get cleaned up. Angelique, you sit down," Soleil commanded in her most authoritarian tone.

At five feet six inches and a hundred and forty pounds of pure pregnancy, she doubted she was all that intimidating, but she'd never had a discipline situation get out of hand in all the five years she'd been running the farm.

Lexie rolled her eyes and stormed out of the room, and Angelique stared after her for a few moments before relenting and sitting down at the table.

Soleil sat opposite her. "Tell me your version of the disagreement," she said calmly.

"She's such a spoiled bitch."

"Without profanity," Soleil added.

"Okay, she's such a spoiled *female canine.*"

Behind all her street attitude, Angelique was wickedly smart.

"Why do you say that?"

She crossed her arms over her chest, slumped in the chair and refused to say anything more.

Soleil leaned forward and put her elbows on the table. "She hurt you, and you wanted to lash out."

Angelique narrowed her eyes. "Don't give me your dumb social-worker strategies."

Soleil sighed. Why hadn't she learned by now?

"Okay, keeping it real," she said in her best south Berkeley accent. "She dissed you, and it pissed you off, which is understandable. But we have to live here together without fighting. Part of this program is learning to work and live cooperatively."

The girl shook her head, sending a cascade of long cornrowed hair, accented with white beads, across her shoulder. "I want to go home."

Was there a full moon? Between the escaped goat, the fighting teenage girls and West showing up out of the blue, Soleil was beginning to feel weary beyond measure. And she wanted ice cream.

"I need you here," she said calmly. "And your neighborhood needs you to go back ready to help run the garden."

"Nobody gives a damn about that stupid garden. I just came here to get out of school."

Soleil tried not to feel insulted by this—Angelique was pushing her buttons. It was no easy feat getting chosen to come to Rainbow Farm. The kids were referred by teachers or social workers, yes, but they still had to show the interest to apply, write a compelling essay to compete for an internship and commit to a year's service in their local garden afterward.

For teenagers who were otherwise usually not salt-of-the-earth nature lovers, this was a huge commitment.

"In your application essay, you said you wanted

to be the change you hoped to see. You said you wanted your neighborhood free of guns and full of healthy kids playing in the street."

Angelique blinked and rolled her eyes, unable to conceal the dampness there all of a sudden. Beneath her tough facade, she was a soft, sensitive girl, full of wide-eyed idealism the likes of which Soleil hadn't seen since she herself had been that young.

"I just made all that crap up," she said weakly.

"I know you and Lexie have some differences. She grew up in a wealthy family and never had to worry about money, while you grew up never knowing if your mom would come home, let alone whether there'd be anything to eat for dinner."

Angelique's face hardened when she looked at Soleil again. "Yeah, so?"

"It can be hard to understand each other when you come from such different upbringings."

"No kidding, Einstein."

"You two will work separately for the rest of the day, and later tonight, once you've both calmed down, I want both of you to talk and work through your disagreement."

Soleil was afraid the girl would stick with the idea of going home, but she was relieved when Angelique simply crossed her arms over her chest and shrugged.

"After you've cleaned up the milk on the floor, you'll go out and help Tonio with the chickens. I think he could use the company."

"Whatever," she answered, then got up and grabbed a towel from the counter to wipe up the mess.

Soleil went in search of Lexie, whom she found lying on her bed upstairs, staring at the ceiling.

"You and Angelique are going to work separately for the rest of the day," she said as she sat on the bed opposite Lexie's.

In response, the girl sighed but said nothing.

"Do you want to tell me your side of what happened?"

"I got sick of her bragging about her rough life and how hard she has it and all that crap."

"You think she was bragging?"

"Yeah, 'cause I'm not *street* enough since I grew up in a nice house and my family has money. She said I might as well be white, for all I know about being black."

Soleil had seen this dynamic of clashing cultures played out before here at the farm, and there wasn't always an easy way to engender respect between kids with vastly different life experiences. But sometimes, with patience, she succeeded.

"I know how it feels to be told I'm not black enough. It hurts."

"Just because I speak using proper English, I'm white? We're never going to have equality when we're racist and judgmental."

Soleil was more intimately familiar with this issue than most people. She'd felt the same pain as a kid.

Having a mother who was a famous poet and a Berkeley professor hadn't done a damn thing for her street cred.

"You know," Soleil said, "my mother is white and my father is black, but we never lived together as a family after I was six years old. So here I was, this girl with black skin being raised by a white woman in Berkeley, living in a white neighborhood. When I went to school, I felt like I had more in common with the white kids, but I so wanted to be accepted by my black peers."

"So what did you do?"

"I tried to be true to myself. I am who I am. I'm not a race, and I'm not a racial identity. I'm an individual. I hung out with the kids who accepted me—and I tried not to get beaten up by the kids who didn't," she said wryly.

Lexie finally smiled. "I bet you got your butt kicked."

"A few times, but I won a few fights of my own."

"I've never been in a fight. Today was the closest I've ever come."

"What made you apply to come here?" Soleil asked.

She remembered what Lexie had written in her application essay, but she wanted to hear the girl's own words. Lexie was her least likely applicant, a resident of the wealthy Oakland hills who attended a prestigious private school. Her life was far removed economically, if not geographically, from the communities where Urban Garden worked to transform empty lots into organic gardens for communities that didn't have easy access to fresh, local produce.

"I don't like driving through bad neighborhoods on the way home and feeling like I'm not a part of the solution to the problems around me. It's like, I'm the opposite of the solution, you know?"

"I don't blame you for feeling that way."

Lexie wasn't interested in being soothed. "It's stupid, because people like Angelique don't even want my help."

"Maybe she does and maybe she doesn't. That doesn't change the fact that we need you as much as we need her."

The girl said nothing as she stared at the ceiling. Stretched out on the bed, her curly black hair was almost dry, and she wore a pink T-shirt in place of the one that had been soaked with milk. Her faded jeans still bore a few milk splatters, and in spite of her simple attire, there was no way for her to disguise the fact that her jeans were expensive, and her T-shirt was designer. She had an elegant polish that made it clear she was an upper-middle-class kid.

Soleil felt her pain, but she couldn't help but sympathize with Angelique, too. It was hard for such an idealistic kid to understand how the world could dole out disparities in life to people who'd done no more than be born to unlucky circumstances.

"Look," Soleil finally said, "I have to go make lunch. You're back on garden duty until lunchtime."

Lexie shrugged as she sat up. "Okay. So long as I'm working alone."

Soleil didn't see any point in arguing now that being at the farm meant working together, whether Lexie wanted to or not. She already knew that, which was why she was so upset in the first place. When she came here, she hadn't bargained on being the only kid from a privileged background, or on being rejected by her peers for that very fact.

As Soleil went back to the kitchen, she allowed her thoughts to stray to West and the impending discussion she'd have to have with him. Her stomach knotted with anxiety.

It was only half past noon, and already she was exhausted. Being pregnant made her want to take a nap every day, and yet her work didn't allow that luxury. So she dealt. But, God, what she wouldn't have given to curl up in bed and shut out the world.

As she passed the rear kitchen window, she could see West walking in from the field, headed right in her direction. Yep, definitely the part of the world she wanted to shut out right now.

PREGNANT, PREGNANT, pregnant, pregnant...

The word would not leave West's head. It loomed there, bigger than any other thought, refusing to get out of the way. Soleil. Pregnant. With *his* baby.

No, he shouldn't have been getting ahead of himself. He needed to wait and hear her story, and trust that if she was really pregnant with his child, she'd have had the decency to tell him right away.

But as soon as that thought formed in his head, he hated the idea of it because it implied that she really was pregnant with someone else's child.

Which was a stupid way to feel since she'd made it clear that she wasn't interested in a relationship with him anyway.

Dammit.

Round and round his thoughts went as he strode across the field. The day had remained gray and misty, though no rain was falling. Not too far away, he could see the teenagers overseeing the goats, and for the briefest moment he experienced a surge of misplaced pride in the work Soleil did. Sure, she was a pie-eyed idealist, but she lived by her ideals every waking moment, and she did good work with the kids.

If he had more time during this leave, he'd love to hang out here and get his hands dirty. But that option didn't seem likely considering the reason why West was on leave. His father had been diagnosed with Alzheimer's disease two months ago, and his mental state had deteriorated drastically in the past six months. Now he needed constant care, but he'd managed to drive away the first three caregivers West had hired, leaving him with no choice but to deal with the situation in person. It was a complicated mess made worse by his complex feelings for his father.

He arrived at the rear door of the farmhouse and knocked.

Soleil called out for him to come in.

As he opened the door, the scent of fresh-baked bread greeted him. He inhaled deeply—he was ravenous.

"Join us for lunch?" Soleil said, though her lack of a smile reminded him that she'd probably prefer he not.

"I will, thanks."

Would she have been inviting him for lunch if she had any big, life-altering news to report?

"We're having sandwiches and potato salad. Hope that's okay."

"Sounds great. Your fence is fixed, by the way."

"Thank you so much. I meant to get out there this morning and totally forgot about it. I've been pretty forgetful lately—it's a side effect of…" She trailed off, seeming to realize too late that she'd brought up something she didn't want to discuss.

"Pregnancy?" he finished for her.

"Yeah." She smiled weakly.

"You look great. Really glowing and healthy."

She rolled her eyes. "Everybody says that. I think it's supposed to make me feel better about my jeans not fitting anymore."

"I always thought you could stand to gain a few

pounds. You were tiny before—you nearly disappeared when you turned sideways."

This conversation between them felt too weird. Last time they'd talked face-to-face, they'd been in a canoe together, having one of their predictable lovers' quarrels, then Soleil had given West a possibly well-deserved shove into the lake and rowed away.

The subject matter of that final argument—motherhood and pregnancy—now seemed eerily timed.

Here they were, five and a half months later, talking like casual acquaintances when what they should have been doing was picking up that conversation where it had left off before she'd abandoned him in the lake.

Too, too weird.

She turned back to the loaf of brown bread she was slicing on the counter.

"How can I help?" West asked as he went to the sink to wash his hands.

"Whatever you'd like to drink, you can get for yourself from the fridge. You and I can eat first, before I call the kids in."

So she was allowing him a few moments alone with her. Did that mean she was ready to confess the truth? Over sandwiches and potato salad? It didn't exactly sound like Soleil's style.

"How about you? What would you like to drink?" he asked.

"I'll have mineral water. It's in the door of the fridge."

They were still doing the awkward polite small-talk thing, conversing as though they didn't really know each other.

Did they really know each other?

It was hard to say. He felt as if he knew the essence of her. But there had to be a lot he didn't know, such as whether she was a woman with whom he wanted to share a child.

"Listen, Soleil, there's something I need to say."

She stopped what she was doing and looked up at him. "Yes?"

"About last summer—what happened between us, I know we had our conflicts, but I'm willing to put all of that aside."

She leaned against the old Formica counter. Sagged more than leaned, actually. "Okay," she said vaguely.

"Besides, our conflicts were really more about having fun than they were serious disagreements, right?"

She frowned. "That's not how I remember it."

"Oh?"

"I'm a left-leaning organic-farming peacenik, and you're a dedicated member of the military-industrial complex. We had great sex, but that's it."

"Is your beef with me really because I'm in the military?"

"Partly. And it's also because I know you want the traditional married-with-children life, and that makes us inherently incompatible."

West laughed. "You're the one wearing an apron and slicing freshly baked bread, not me."

Her frown turned to a scowl, and West kept a close eye on the bread knife just to be safe.

"You're not funny," she said, her voice flat.

"Oh, and *you're* pregnant with a child."

My child, he almost said.

"But I'm not married, and I never will be. I don't believe in it."

They'd have to wait and see about that. If she was carrying his child, they'd be talking commitment. He didn't see any harm in a shotgun marriage, if the situation called for it. And in spite of all her big talk, he'd have bet the sun and moon she was damn scared of raising a child alone.

It was time to find out the truth—pleasantries be dammed. Speculation was counterproductive. Only with the facts could he make a solid plan for the future.

"Soleil is there something you need to tell me about your pregnancy?"

CHAPTER THREE

SOLEIL FELT as if the words were lodged in her throat, refusing to exit. A wave of nausea the likes of which she hadn't felt in weeks hit her, and her face broke out in a cold sweat.

West was not a man she wanted to raise a child with. She'd yet to meet anyone she wanted to raise a child with, but especially not a trained killer, whose politics and values were as opposite hers as they could possibly be.

Despite that, he deserved the truth.

"Yes," she said, her mouth too dry.

No sooner did she speak than the nausea turned into a very real need to throw up. This wasn't morning sickness—that had gone away around the twelve-week mark—it was a full-blown case of nerves.

Covering her mouth, she darted across the kitchen and down the hallway to the bathroom, and bent over the toilet just in time to lose it.

West followed her. She felt his hand on her back then, and he was holding her pigtails away from her face as she vomited.

When she was finished, he said, "That was pretty spectacular."

"Shut up," she mumbled.

She went to the sink and rinsed her mouth, then wiped her face.

She took a few deep, steadying breaths, then turned to face West again. But she couldn't quite meet his gaze in this small, claustrophobic space. Instead, she edged past him and went into the living room, where she dropped to the couch and put her face in her hands.

West followed, and she could feel the couch sag as he sat next to her.

She could feel the tension in the air so thick it was hard to breathe, and she had to break it now before she suffocated. He was a good man, regardless of their differences. He didn't deserve this.

She looked him in the eyes again.

"It's your baby," she said quietly.

Worry transformed into understanding, and he exhaled loudly, leaning back against the couch as he did so. But his hands, one on each thigh, remained tense.

"You're sure?"

"Of course I'm sure," she said.

"You're sure." This time, a statement instead of a question.

Soleil watched the storm of emotions in his gaze, and she grew more terrified by the second. Before she could come up with any lame excuses for not having told him sooner, he stood and looked as if he might explode.

"What the hell, Soleil? What the *hell?* You didn't tell me? You were just going to go on your merry way without letting the other parent in the situation know this key piece of information? It didn't freaking occur to you that the father might like to know he's the father?"

"I—I—"

"You thought maybe you could slip this one by me?"

His voice was too loud now, nearly a shout, and Soleil was painfully aware of all the adolescent ears nearby that could be hearing the argument.

"Could you please lower your voice? The kids—"

"Oh, what, *now* you're worried about being a good role model?"

"That's not fair."

"You don't need your *baby daddy?* Is that it? Is that what you tell the kids here?"

She winced at his bad imitation of a street accent. Any other time, she'd have given him an earful for that kind of comment, but now she didn't have any room to talk—not literally or figuratively.

"West—" she said as calmly as she could, but he was closing the distance between them now, and panic rose in her chest.

"It's crap!" he said, in her face now, close enough that she could inhale his woodsy scent. "You don't do this to people. This is utter crap!"

She didn't have any right to lose her temper now. It was his turn, and she had to take whatever he doled out. She owed him that. So she bit her tongue.

"You're right," she said. "I'm sorry."

Her apology seemed to take the wind out of his sails. His shoulders slumped, and he retreated a step.

Shaking his head, he said, "How could you? How could you do this? How could you keep this from me?"

"I wanted to tell you in person. I'm sorry it's taken so long."

"You wanted to tell me in person," he repeated numbly. "All this time, you didn't even call me."

"I'm sorry. I'm really sorry."

"I think this warranted a phone call before now," he said.

He didn't sound calm so much as he sounded defeated. West Morgan, in the time she'd known him, had never sounded defeated. In fact, part of what had made her so willing to spar with him was that he'd seemed undefeatable.

"You're right. I kept putting off deciding how to tell you, another day, then another and another until all of a sudden there you were driving down the road toward my goat."

His expression turned wounded. "Did you really plan to tell me?"

Busted.

Her mouth went dry, and she worked to find the ability to speak again.

"Honestly, I wasn't sure what to do. I knew it would be wrong to keep it from you, but I…I put off deciding. That's the truth."

"Okay."

She could see him processing the information, trying to decide on his next course of action, which was what she feared most.

Captain West Morgan would have a very narrow idea of the right way to handle this situation. Get married. Settle down. Make the best of it. She'd become the target of his next mission: Operation Family.

With the echoes of their last argument and his 1950s clichés ringing in her head, she had no interest in becoming a cozy family of three. She had no interest in any of the things that would entail—the compromises, the subjugation, the loss of freedom.

"I decided on my own to have the baby, and I don't expect anything from you. Just so you know." Though she knew these words were wasted and unnecessary.

"Of course I'm going to be involved," he said.

"Of course," she echoed weakly.

"I'm the father. I won't let my own child grow up without a father."

He looked stunned but determined, and Soleil knew she wasn't going to convince him of anything now. But she couldn't help standing her ground—she was just as unyielding as he when it came to her ideals.

"You live in Colorado, and I live in California. So

what? You're going to commute here to do diaper duty and midnight feedings?"

"I don't know what I'm going to do. You've had months to think about this, and I've had a couple of minutes."

Right. It wasn't fair of her to be sticking it to him now.

"Maybe I should skip lunch and go," he continued. "We've both got a lot to think about."

She cast a glance at him, so much larger than her, so much more male. So foreign, so other…

He both intrigued and repelled her, even now. She wanted to run away from him, and she wanted to reach out and knead the tension from his shoulders.

"I'll be around. You've got my number," she said. "Feel free to call if you want to discuss this further."

His posture, beneath the gray wool fisherman's sweater he wore, remained slumped. She hated to acknowledge that she'd been the one to take that toll on him. Even at her best, she'd never felt as if she'd beaten him. Until now. It was a bitter win, if it could even be called that.

He turned to go, and as she watched him walk toward the door, she had a bewildering urge to grab hold of him and beg him not to leave. But she didn't.

Of course not.

It wasn't in her vocabulary to ask for help.

Except now, walking out the door was the man

she had a sneaking sense of dread she might need, whether she wanted to need him or not.

JULIA MORGAN had never set out to try online dating.

And as she sat in the Guerneville coffee shop, nervously scanning the passersby outside the window for a familiar face, she could hardly recall why it had ever seemed like a good idea.

It had all sort of, well…happened. First came the laptop computer her three sons had given her for her birthday. She'd never been a computer person, and she didn't really see the need for it since she'd managed to teach for thirty years without one.

Then came her newfound love of e-mail. Who knew it could be so much fun. Instant communication with her friends, children and grandchildren. It was almost too good to be true. She could even get pictures of them on the computer, just like in all those commercials.

And, she'd figured out how to upload the pictures to the Internet and order prints from a Web site.

Amazing.

But that was what had led to the whole online-dating embarrassment. She didn't dare tell anyone, because who would approve? Certainly not her friends, most of whom were either married, or if they were divorced like her, they were content or resigned to being alone. And she couldn't tell her kids, who'd likely worry about her or decide it was time she move in with one of them for closer supervision.

Really, it had started so innocently. She'd acciden-tally clicked on an online-dating ad a few weeks ago, and before she knew it, she was putting in her zip code and looking through a list of single men her age. Then a little box had popped up telling her that all she had to do was upload her own photo, fill out a profile form, and she'd be able to contact any man she wanted.

She'd immediately turned off the whole computer and went to do some gardening, horrified at herself for even considering such a thing.

But there was one man she hadn't been able to stop thinking about.

His screen name, letsbefrank, had made her smile for no particular reason, and she'd very much liked his eyes—kind and brown, the sort of eyes that looked right at you, in, well…a frank expression.

Turns out, his real name was actually Frank Fiorelli, and he was now late for the meet-for-coffee date they'd scheduled after exchanging e-mails.

Okay, maybe he wasn't actually late. Julia couldn't remember if she'd set her silver watch five minutes fast the way she did the clocks in her house, and being the perpetually early person she was, she'd gotten to the coffee shop a full half hour before the date. So, she'd been waiting a while, growing more and more anxious as each second ticked by.

Her green-tea latte, neglected on the table, was still full. She took a sip and discovered it had cooled to room temperature.

Then a buzzing sound came from her purse—the cell phone set to vibrate so as not to interrupt her coffee date—and she let out a sigh of relief, thinking it must be Frank calling to cancel.

Which would be great, since she now understood from her terrible case of nerves that she wasn't cut out for this Internet-dating stuff after all.

But the name on the cell phone's little screen was West, her middle son.

She answered with a tense-sounding hello.

"Hey, Mom," he said.

Was it her imagination, or did he sound a little distressed, too?

"Oh, West, honey, how are you?"

"I just got into town, actually."

"What?" Julia blinked in surprise. "Today? I thought you weren't arriving for two more weeks."

A pause, during which she wondered if he'd somehow discovered her Internet dallying.

"It's Dad," he finally said, his voice tight.

Julia had been divorced from the General long enough that mention of his name didn't evoke any particular emotion, but she certainly didn't wish him any harm, and her stomach flip-flopped at West's tone.

"What is it? Is he okay?"

"He's having some problems I need to deal with in person," he answered vaguely. Julia knew for sure something was wrong, but she decided it was better not to push.

West would tell her the whole story when he was ready. But her mother radar was picking up signals. Something was definitely wrong, with the General, or West, or both.

"Will you be staying with me? Can you come for dinner tonight?"

Her gaze fell on a tall, well-built man with close-cropped gray hair and kind brown eyes, headed toward her, and she barely heard what her son said next.

"I need to stay with Dad for now, but I may want to move to your guest room once I've got him squared away. And I'd love to have dinner with you, but I'll have to let you know later, if that's okay."

"Sure, dear," she said hurriedly. "I have to go now. Talk to you soon. Bye-bye."

She hung up on the sound of her son's befuddled "Oh, okay, talk to you la—"

Then Julia tucked the phone in her bag and took a deep breath in a failed effort to soothe her jangled nerves.

Frank Fiorelli was standing inside the doorway of the coffee shop now, looking around for her. His gaze swept in her direction, and she smiled tentatively at him.

She hadn't felt this keyed up, frantic and nervous since her early twenties—the last time she'd been on the dating scene, she realized with some chagrin.

Dear Lord.

He was walking toward her now, his confident

stride a stark contrast to the shaky feeling that had overtaken her.

First impression—she liked him. The lines on his face were all smile lines, as if he'd spent a lifetime in a good mood, and it had the effect of making him seem as though he was smiling even when he wasn't.

She stood when he reached her table.

"Frank?" she said, feeling like a ridiculous schoolgirl.

He smiled broadly, revealing a set of white, healthy teeth that looked real. Never a thing to take for granted in the over-fifty crowd.

"You must be Julia."

She was about to extend her hand for a handshake when he leaned in and gave her a brief, friendly hug. This could have been awkward or even creepy, but he managed to make it feel utterly natural, and Julia found herself charmed already.

"I'm going to grab a cup of coffee. Can I get you anything while I'm at the counter?" he asked.

"Oh, no." She cast a glance at her now-cold cup of tea. "I'm fine."

He grinned again, and she thought she detected the slightest hint of nervousness, which made her feel a little more at ease. He was human, like her.

She sat and took advantage of the chance to stare at Frank as he waited to place his order, his back to her. He wore a sage-green T-shirt tucked into a pair of worn khaki pants, a small braided leather belt that also seemed to have lived a long and well-loved life. On his feet were a pair of brown leather thong sandals, revealing tanned skin and well-shaped toes.

The whole effect was casual, relaxed, unpretentious… Nice.

Her gaze returned to his broad shoulders, solid and strong, tapering to a narrow waist. He looked like a man who stayed in shape, and she remembered his online profile, which had read like an itinerary at an outdoor-adventure resort—kayaking, hiking, surfing, biking…

Could Julia keep up? She managed to stay fit between her daily yoga practice, a pilates class twice a week, long walks and hikes and religiously working in her garden, but she was no extreme-sports person. Not by a long shot.

Heck, she wasn't even sure what *extreme sports* meant.

Oh, well, at the age of fifty-eight, she was as happy as she could be with her body, and she wasn't about to worry for more than a moment about how Frank Fiorelli would feel about her physique. She was strong and healthy and still looked nice in a pair of jeans, and if he wasn't happy with that, he could keep right on looking.

Yet another glorious thing about aging—the loss of the crippling self-consciousness of youth.

Frank returned to the table with coffee in hand, sat across from Julia and grinned again. "So," he said.

"You're even prettier than your photo. Too bad you can't say the same about me."

She laughed, grateful for the joke to break the ice.

"You're the first person I've met online," she confessed.

"Really?"

She nodded. "It's even stranger than I thought it would be."

"Can I make a confession, too?"

Oh, dear. "Sure."

"My daughter signed me up on the site without my knowing it."

"No!"

He shook his head, smiling ruefully. "She told me about it afterward, said I might start getting e-mail from ladies interested in going on dates with me."

"And?"

"I thought, am I so pathetic my daughter needs to intervene in my personal life?"

"I wouldn't say that's pathetic. It's kind of sweet, actually. Like an older version of *Sleepless in Seattle*."

"Anyway, I figured I'd better log onto the Web site and see what the heck she'd gotten me into, and before I could stop myself I was looking at your profile and e-mailing you."

"Wow. I'm the first person you contacted?"

"The only one. When I saw that self-deprecating smile of yours, I knew there had to be something special about you. Not many people could communicate so much with one facial expression. But you…it's all written right there on your face."

Julia blushed. She'd been told before that she wore her emotions on her sleeve, but she'd never quite gotten used to the fact that she could be so easily read.

"Self-deprecation is underrated," Frank said. "A person who knows how to laugh at herself is a person I want to call my friend."

"I'm glad you e-mailed me," Julia said. "I heard from a bunch of men. It was kind of bewildering to get all that e-mail once I signed up on the site."

"What made you join?"

She laughed. "Foolishness, mostly. I clicked on one of those ads by accident, and next thing I knew, I was looking at your profile."

"It wasn't foolishness—it was fate."

"That sounds far more romantic than my version of it."

He sipped his coffee. They'd already done a lot of the getting-to-know-you conversation via e-mail and phone, which, Julia realized now, was probably a mistake. It left them with less to talk about face-to-face.

"I was thinking, maybe you'd like to take a walk after this?" Frank said finally.

"Where to?"

"I do a little sculpting. I have a studio down the street. I don't normally bring people to it, so it's a mess, but something tells me you might enjoy it.

Also, my wily daughter will be there, so you can meet the person responsible for *our* having met."

"Sure, that sounds lovely. Why don't we go now. These are portable," she said, nodding at the paper cups.

"Great. Let's go."

They left the coffee shop, then headed north along a side street. The day was sunnier here than it had been in Promise, and Julia breathed in the fresh, crisp air, enjoying looking at the funky shops they passed along the way.

Frank's gait was casual and not too hurried. He made a point of keeping the conversation rolling along, telling her anecdotes about the town of Guerneville, and Julia was grateful since she still felt too nervous to think straight.

A few minutes later, they were standing in front of a brown-shingled building with large windows and a sharply pitched roof. The first floor of the building was a business called the Green Gallery.

"This is my place. My daughter runs the gallery, and I work upstairs in the loft."

"Oh." Julia blinked at the news, as she quickly re-formed her mental picture of Frank as retired engineer and all-around outdoorsman to…sculptor and art-gallery owner? He had a few surprises up his sleeve. She hoped his artwork wasn't awful, so she could find something nice to say about it without lying.

"Come on in and meet Chloe."

Julia followed him into the light, clean space of the gallery. Polished bamboo floors gleamed, and the white walls bounced light around so much that overhead lights were barely necessary.

"Hey, Pop," said a slender, pretty, dark-haired woman who looked to be in her late twenties.

She glanced curiously from Frank to Julia, smiling warmly.

"Chloe, this is my friend Julia Morgan. She lives over at Promise Lake. I thought I'd show her around the gallery and studio."

"Great. I just finished putting up the new stuff."

"Chloe was an art history major in college. Poor girl can't get a real job so she has to work for me."

Chloe rolled her eyes at this. "Don't believe a word he says."

"Actually, I'm lucky to have her," he confessed. "She had a choice between working at a prestigious gallery in San Francisco, or staying here in backwater Guerneville to help out her old pa."

"It wasn't such a hard choice. Dad lets me do whatever I want with this place, so I get to display the work of environmentally conscious artists. Most of the works here are made entirely with recycled materials."

"That's wonderful," Julia said as her gaze landed on a dazzling installation of brightly colored smashed aluminum cans.

At first the piece looked to be made out of something else entirely, and Julia wouldn't have guessed about the cans until she heard the words *recycled materials.*

"And she tells me what I'm doing wrong with my works in progress," Frank added in a teasing tone. "She's a brutal critic."

"Dad's ridiculously modest," Chloe said. "He'll never tell you that he's one of the pioneers of green art."

"Oh?"

"He started working with recycled materials in the early seventies, when green was still just a color."

"He never mentioned…" Julia said.

"He's pretty good." Chloe smiled. "You'll see."

"Remember, she's trying to get me a date. C'mon," Frank said, nodding toward a door in the back of the room. "I'll show you my studio."

Julia followed him up a flight of stairs. The second floor was a wide-open space filled with soft light from the wall of windows on one side of the room. The other walls were wood, giving the place a warm glow. A large table was littered with various tools and pieces of odd materials. In the center of the room stood a metal sculpture—a meticulously crafted globe that, upon closer inspection, Julia could see was a representation of the earth.

"It's beautiful," she said.

"I'm afraid it's a bit too masculine. Nature and earth should feel more feminine, don't you think?"

Julia gave the matter some thought. "Maybe you're right."

"Perhaps you can help me figure out how to fix it."

She laughed. "I'm a retired elementary school teacher. Most of my art expertise involves pasting macaroni to construction paper."

"You're being modest."

She turned her attention to a finished sculpture in the corner, a piece that looked a bit like a bird in flight. It was both stark and stunning.

"That's my raven," Frank said. "What do you think?"

"Very striking. What's it made of?"

"Old bicycle tires, meticulously cut into tiny pieces."

And as she got closer, she could see it was true. The tread patterns had the effect of looking like the texture of feathers.

"I used to sculpt with traditional materials, but one day I looked around and thought, 'Why am I putting more garbage out there in the world, when there's already so much discarded stuff the planet's nearly drowning in it?'"

Julia looked at him, impressed that a man of their generation could be so aware of his own environmental impact. Every other man she'd known over fifty was too busy driving his giant SUV to the golf course or jetting off on vacation, to worry about such things.

Heck, *she* hardly worried about such things, comfortable as she was in her safe middle-class life. Here was a man who devoted his art to making important political statements. Was she political enough for him, or would he ultimately decide she was bourgeois and dull?

This was ridiculous. She was too old to be so worried about impressing a man.

She looked at Frank and realized he'd been watching her brood. "I know this isn't the cheeriest stuff. What do you say we get out of here and take a stroll downtown?"

"Oh, thank you, but I should probably be getting home soon."

The wind had been taken out of her sails. She suddenly had the feeling something was very wrong, and she was wasting her time here with this Frank person. Feeling self-conscious again, she took a sip of tea to have something to do with her mouth.

"I know how you feel, Julia—like we're too old for this online-dating stuff. Maybe too old for dating at all, right?"

She smiled, feeling her cheeks redden that he'd managed to read her mind so easily.

"Maybe we are," he continued. "But what if we aren't? What if we miss out on something wonderful by thinking like that?"

She looked at him again, at the way his eyes crinkled at the corners, and she remembered why she'd wanted to meet him in the first place—because he seemed like a good man. Because he seemed like someone she might be able to care about.

He still did. He had a daughter who clearly liked him, and he had what looked so far like a vibrant, interesting life.

"What do you say we meet for dinner later this week?" she blurted before she could lose her nerve.

"I'd like that."

"I'll call you to make plans?"

"I'll look forward to it," he said.

Whatever else was wrong—with West, or her ex-husband or her own ability to seize the day—she couldn't let it ruin this one little grasp she'd made at trying to find happiness a second time around.

CHAPTER FOUR

WEST DROVE to his father's house in a half rage, half stupor. The news that he was going to be a father was only partly sinking in.

It scared the hell out of him. If he'd just learned he'd have to have a leg amputated, he'd at least have begun immediately to see all the ways that news would impact him, but this…

Becoming a father, so unexpectedly, and with a woman he had no significant relationship with, seemed like someone had detonated a nuclear bomb in the middle of his life. Existence as he knew it had been blown to smithereens, and he was a stunned survivor, wandering around unable yet to make sense of the aftermath. What did it mean for his career—where, until now, he'd only had himself to consider when accepting assignments and promotions? Would he have to limit the postings he was eligible for? Would he even be able to continue in the military? If not, what the hell would he do? This was the only job he knew, the only one he'd ever wanted.

As he pulled into the driveway of his family home,

he forcibly put aside the dilemma for a while. He had a whole other set of devastating circumstances to face, although at least he came here expecting bad news.

He got out of the SUV and strode up the sidewalk, his dread growing with each step. As he reached the door, he could hear his father yelling inside. General Morgan—or the General, as he was usually referred to—was prone to yelling, but the bellowing he was engaged in now had a different timber, almost manical quality, that West had only started to recognize last summer during his most recent visit home.

West had never imagined his own father succumbing to any weakness, let alone weakness of the mind. The tone of his father's voice sounded crazy. No, that wasn't the right word. *Senile* was better. The most accurate description, according to the doctors, was Alzheimer's disease.

And it wasn't early onset, either. No, the General was advanced into the dementia that was making him more and more incompetent, less and less able to function as a normal person.

"I said I don't own a goddamn cat!" he bellowed again. "Get that animal out of my house!"

This urged West to take a step forward, until he was knocking hard on the front door.

A moment later, an exasperated-looking woman in a white outfit opened it.

"Hi," West said. "You must be Margie from the temp service?"

"I am," she said. "And if you'll excuse me—"

She was cut off by the sound of a yowl, then the cat scrambling through the front door and flying across the porch in a blur.

"Mr. Morgan, I won't have you abusing that animal!" she said as she disappeared into the house.

West stepped inside. To the left, he could see the double doors of the study were open, and his father was standing there, brandishing a cane.

"Never have liked cats," he muttered, ignoring Margie.

His gaze landed on West. "Who's that? West?" he said. "What're you doing here?"

Relief flooded West. At least his father recognized him still, if not the cat.

"Hey, Dad. Remember I said I'd be arriving here today?"

"Oh, sure." But he didn't look as though he remembered.

"I'll be going now, if that's okay with you, sir," Margie announced. "Mr. Morgan has been making it clear all morning that he doesn't want me in the house."

West followed her into the kitchen, where she retrieved a coat hanging on the back of a chair.

"Thank you so much for sticking around until I could get here," he said, pulling out his wallet to give her a tip.

"Heaven knows I understand how dementia patients are—I've been working with them for twenty years. I simply don't tolerate any outright abuse of the animals in the house. Me, I'm trained to defend myself, but that poor cat doesn't understand what's going on."

"I hope he hasn't been too hard on you."

Her lips went thin. "Have you been around an Alzheimer's patient before?"

"I visited here last summer, but he was only forgetful then."

"Sometimes they go downhill fast, and it's a real shame to see. You'd best be prepared for him being a lot more than forgetful."

Margie had only been with his dad for a few days. The General had been so alternately belligerent and obscene with every caregiver that none would stick around for longer than a few weeks.

"What kind of trouble have you had with him?"

"You just witnessed the incident with that poor cat. He's been insisting all day that the animal doesn't live here."

"So that's how he is all the time?"

"Not all the time. The thing with Alzheimer's is, it comes in waves. For a while he'll be living in the past, convinced it's 1963 or he's in the middle of the war or his wife's been gone to the grocery store too long. Then he'll take a nap and wake up normal."

"What should I do when he's confused and agitated?"

"Sometimes it's best to play along and save yourself the battle. Other times, like if he might do something to hurt himself or someone else, you're going to have to let him know he's confused, and that's where the battle begins."

"Is there any chance I can convince you to stick around at least for another week or so? It'll be an easier job when I'm around to act as a buffer."

"I don't think—"

"I'll make sure there's a nice holiday bonus for you."

Anything to keep him from having to be here alone all the time with his dad. He wasn't sure how he'd manage as it was.

Margie sighed. "I've got to go to a dental appointment this afternoon, but I suppose I can stick around here for another week or two if Mr. Morgan behaves himself."

"Thank you so much."

Whew. That bought him some time, at least.

She picked up her purse from the table, accepted the tip from West and headed for the door.

She paused in the door of the study. "Goodbye, Mr. Morgan. I'll be going now that your son is here to look out for you this afternoon."

"I already told you to go. Now get out of—"

"Dad!"

Margie gave West a significant look, then walked out the front door, the determined set of her shoulders speaking volumes as she let the screen door slam behind her.

West turned to his dad. "You can't chase away every caregiver I hire, Dad."

"I don't need any *caregiver.* I'm a grown man, not a drooling baby in diapers." He banged his cane on the floor to emphasize the point, then walked over to his desk chair and took a seat.

"Did you hit your cat with the cane?"

"That cat? I've never seen it before, and it sure as hell doesn't belong in this house. Your mother's allergic, you know."

"But—" West was about to say that his mother didn't live here anymore, except he wasn't sure it would do any good to point it out right now.

Hadn't Margie said he should choose his battles? So long as the cat was outside, they had time to see if his father would return to the present day and remember that his beloved pet for the past decade actually did belong there.

His father turned on the radio next to his desk and adjusted the volume on a talk show, then settled back in his chair to listen.

Some welcome home.

"Hey, Dad, I'm going to make a few phone calls, then maybe we can have a cup of coffee and catch up."

"Eh? Can you be quiet? I'm listening to my show right now."

Right.

West closed the front door and locked it, then went into the kitchen again. He put a pot of coffee on, noticing at every turn signs of decay. The house was no longer the pristine home his mother once kept, but that was nothing new.

The divorce long past, his father, in spite of his talk of high standards, had been letting things slide in his bachelor years. Two more wives had come and gone, each less patient and less forgiving than Julia Morgan had been, and with the crumbling of each marriage, the General had seemed a little less like his former stickler self.

It was as if he didn't have the energy to be the man in command of every detail anymore, as evidenced by cobwebs in the corners and a thin coating of grime on the stove top.

"Women's work," his father had always said of housekeeping—far out of his element in a post-feminist world.

West, on the other hand, considered keeping a home in good order a fact of life. It was simply part of being an adult. So he grabbed the duster from the cleaning caddy that had always been stored under the sink and got rid of the cobwebs, then gave the stove top a good scrubbing. Once he'd completed those tasks, he felt a little more at ease in the room and sat at the table to call his mother.

He wanted to hear a normal voice right now, one that didn't have any bad news to bear. Because as soon as he stopped thinking about his father, thoughts of Soleil being pregnant took over.

He was going to be a father, for better or worse. He was going to be responsible for a child in less than four months. And here was his own father, turning into a two-hundred-pound belligerent child.

Would West be able to cope? Would he be a better father than his own dad had been?

Somehow, he would have to be.

JULIA DIDN'T LIKE the look on her middle son's face. Something was definitely wrong, to have him looking so troubled and showing up at such an odd time of year, too. Normally West arrived in town like clockwork for the holidays, the weekend before Christmas—not weeks ahead of time.

"Can I get you a glass of cabernet?" she asked as he sat at the breakfast bar across from her.

She had her hands immersed in a tossed salad, trying to coax the grape tomatoes back to the top of the pile of vegetables.

"Why don't I get it? You'll have one, too?" he said, standing and heading for the wine rack before she could stop him.

"Sure. There's already a bottle breathing over by the fridge."

Having one of her children here in her post-divorce condo always felt a little odd to her, even after all these years. Some silly part of her thought they were only supposed to be together as a family at the house she and John had bought after he'd retired from the military. They'd lived in the house as a family for maybe the last five or six years of the marriage, but in her head, she'd imagined all their family get-togethers from then on out happening at that grand old Craftsman. That was before she'd accepted that the marriage was over and somehow she couldn't shake the image.

Here in her little condo, which had become her refuge from the ugliness of her marriage, her children felt like reminders of the ways in which she'd failed. And that was a notion she'd never, ever speak out loud.

"So what's new with you?" he asked as he prepared the drinks.

Oh, the usual. Online dating, meeting up with strange men, et cetera.

She bit her lip to keep from grinning. Sometimes she could hardly believe her own nerve. Would she dare tell West what she'd done?

Not right now.

"I've been volunteering for the literacy program at the library, doing some knitting, yoga, hiking… Oh, and I'll have to introduce you to the new rabbits I'm fostering. They're confined to the garage until they learn better potty manners."

West set her glass of wine beside her, and she realized she was rambling. Possibly sounding guilty.

"Keeping busy as always," he said, lifting his glass.

She took hers and toasted. "To surprise visits from my children."

"I'm sorry I didn't give you more notice. This was kind of a last-minute thing."

His tense expression returned as he paused and took a drink.

"What's going on, West?"

"It's Dad," he said. "He's been diagnosed with Alzheimer's disease."

The news struck Julia dumb for a moment. She swallowed her wine and struggled to wrap her mind around the idea. Her ex-husband, the father of her children, the invincible General she'd both loved and hated for more years than she could count, never got sick.

He was too ornery to get sick.

But it was as she'd feared when she'd heard West's voice earlier over the phone.

"Oh…" She set down her glass, put her hand over her mouth.

"It's progressed faster than I thought it would. In a matter of months he's gone from being forgetful to downright belligerent and disoriented."

"Oh…"

Now she was repeating herself like an idiot. She needed to come up with something helpful to say, but she was shocked senseless.

"Mom, sit down." West took her by the elbow, guiding her out of the kitchen and into the family room.

She lowered herself onto the couch, and he sat next to her.

"Do you need some water?"

"Alzheimer's disease," she murmured, the diagnosis sounding completely absurd to her ears still.

West went to the kitchen, filled a glass with tap water and brought it to her. She took a halfhearted sip and set the glass aside.

"I know it's a shock. It's taken me a while to accept it myself. And I really thought we'd have more time before he'd get so…bad."

"Who's caring for him?" Julia finally found the sense to ask.

"We've had home-health nurses coming in for the past few months, but he keeps chasing them off. That's why I moved up my vacation time—so I could come here and try to get him some reliable care."

"You've known about this since the summer and haven't told me? Your brothers have known? No one's said a word."

"I'm sorry. I wasn't ready to talk about it, and we all thought we had more time."

"Oh, dear Lord, West. I'm so sorry, too. I never thought I'd live to see the day your father couldn't take care of himself."

There. She'd said something appropriate, something sympathetic, but it didn't begin to reveal the torrent of feelings threatening to choke her right now.

From the kitchen a buzzer sounded, reminding her that the tri-tip roast was done. "Let me get that before it burns," she said as she stood and headed for the other room.

"Need some help?"

"Sure, I think we could use the distraction. Can you chop some mushrooms?"

West rummaged in the fridge while she took the roast out of the oven, grateful for a chance to process the news about her ex-husband for a moment in private.

John.

Not her ex-husband. His name was John, and it was high time she let go of the past, wasn't it?

She hadn't ever been one to dwell there, but now she saw that John as he was at the time they divorced had become frozen in her mind. To her, he was still the same arrogant, forceful, infuriating man, the same age—ten years her senior—same appearance…

They didn't see each other often. Promise, with a population over seven thousand, was just big enough to keep an ex-husband from underfoot. She might see him in passing once or twice a year, and the last time had been nearly a year ago at her oldest son's house, when John had been arriving as she was leaving. He'd seemed normal then, strong and unyielding as ever.

Alzheimer's disease…

The feelings finally caught in her throat, and she dropped the pot holder next to the roasting pan on the stove and excused herself to the bathroom.

Once inside the guest bath, she burst into silent, heaving tears.

This made no sense. She didn't love John anymore, did she? She didn't miss him—never had in all the years they'd been apart.

But she had, once upon a time, loved him enough to think they'd spend their whole lives together, right up until the end. She'd once believed their marriage vows with all her heart, and when she'd imagined their future, she had often pictured them growing old together, keeping each other company in their final years. She'd believed they would take care of each other in their old age.

Wasn't that one of the reasons for marrying? Wasn't it a benefit of all the trouble, heartache and compromise?

And here they were, in their so-called golden years, alone. Not taking care of each other at all, but instead, virtual strangers trying not to peer in the windows of each other's lives.

This, unexpectedly, hurt like hell.

She had to pull herself together before West started wondering what was wrong. She dabbed her wet eyes with toilet paper, blew her nose, then looked in the mirror to see how wrecked she was. Blotchy skin, red nose, glassy eyes.

Good thing she kept a spare bag of makeup in here. She touched herself up then headed back to the kitchen to face her son.

She was being terribly selfish, worrying so much about her own feelings when her sons were the ones who would suffer the most. They were losing their father right before their eyes. West, the most sensitive of all the boys—though he'd die to have it pointed out—would be hit hardest of all. *Had* been hit hardest, whether he realized it yet or not.

She needed to be strong for him.

In the kitchen, he was standing in front of the stove, his head bent as he peered into a skillet. His profile had looked the same his entire life. Even when he'd first come out of her womb, she had a frozen image of his newborn baby head in profile, same as it was today. Strong brow and nose, wide, observant eyes staring out at the world....

"Hey, I hope you wanted these mushrooms sautéed," West said when he looked over at her. "They're almost done."

"Oh, thank you." She turned her attention to the salad.

"Hey, Mom?"

"Yes?"

"The stuff about Dad, it's not the only big news I have."

Julia's stomach knotted. This was West, the one who tried so hard to please her and his father. It wasn't like him to bring bad news.

"What is it?"

His expression wavered somewhere between grim and hopeful.

Oh, dear.

"Do you remember Soleil Freeman? The woman I was seeing in the summer?"

"Of course I know Soleil—she's in my book group. She's lovely."

"She is, yeah. I'm glad you like her because she's going to be a bigger part of our lives in the future."

Oh?

"Well, that's a good thing, I hope?"

West still looked grim. "I'm not sure if you know she's pregnant."

"She is?"

"Yes, five and a half months along."

"I hadn't heard. Maybe that's why she hasn't been to the book group lately."

"Mom…" His face paled. "I'm the father of the baby."

Julia almost didn't comprehend what he was saying. She took the news as if he was telling her he was the prime minister of Neptune.

"But…how…"

No, that was ridiculous to say. Of course she knew *how*. She just didn't know how her eminently responsible son could be saying these words to her now.

Then it struck her. This was life. Bad things happened to good people, and good things happened to good people, and this… This news—Soleil and West having a baby together—regardless of the how or why of it, was one of the *good* things.

Julia smiled, closed the distance between herself and her son and embraced him.

"Congratulations, West. I'm very happy for you—for all of us."

West hugged her back stiffly, then pulled away to look into her eyes. "Really?"

"Of course I am. It's a baby! What could be happier than that?"

He shook his head. "I'm still in shock. I don't know how to feel."

She took his hand in hers and gave it a few pats. "How long have you known about the baby?"

"I found out today."

"I'm glad you told me right away. I needed some good news."

"Yeah," he said, looking paler by the second.

"This is quite a shock for you, isn't it?"

West put down the spatula, turned off the burner and slumped against the counter. The last of his ability to hold himself together had finally been chipped away, apparently, because his expression was grimmer than she'd seen it in years.

"That's an understatement," he said, sounding more lighthearted than he looked.

"I suppose she wanted to deliver the news in person, and that's why she didn't let you know sooner?"

West shook his head. "I have no idea. I'm furious that she didn't tell me right away, and I'm…I'm in shock."

"Of course you are." Julia took her son by the arm. "Why don't you sit? I'll get our dinner on some plates so we can eat."

He returned to the counter and sat, then took a drink of his wine.

"Just remember, she's probably terrified. Being pregnant alone is no easy road to travel."

"She doesn't have to be alone," he said defensively.

"No, but that's not how it feels to her right now. She's the one with the baby growing inside her." But this wasn't what West needed to hear right now.

Julia bit her lip and tried to think what her son *did* need to hear.

He glared at his wineglass and said nothing.

"West, you know, I'm going to be here to support you no matter what. Why don't you tell me what's really going on?"

He shook his head. "I wish I knew."

"You and Soleil—I didn't think you were continuing your relationship."

"Well, we weren't. Or I mean, we aren't, exactly. I really don't know what's going to happen, but…"

"You really like her, don't you?"

"I do, and I'm thinking we should raise the child together, if she's willing."

From what Julia knew of Soleil, that was a big *if*. She was one of the most fiercely independent, unconventional women Julia had ever met, and her comments during their discussion of Kate Chopin's classic *The Awakening* made it clear she considered drowning the happiest ending possible for the female main character who faced being unhappily trapped in a marriage.

"That's a lovely sentiment. Are you sure?" Julia said gently.

"I *am*." He gave her one of those looks reminiscent of the teen years, meant to communicate that she was out of her mind.

"I only mean to suggest, Soleil's a strong-willed woman with her own mind about things. You may want to consider taking your time, letting this news sink in, before charging ahead with a plan of action."

"I know, Mom. I know. I simply can't imagine the thought of my own child growing up without me there to help raise him or her."

"And that's a beautiful thing about you, West."

He shrugged, as if to shake off her compliment. She knew her son better than he realized. And she knew he wouldn't settle for anything less than a hero's effort in this situation.

But sometimes, what was called for was more finesse and thoughtfulness, instead of a soldier's boldness.

"Just go slowly. This is big, life-altering stuff, but you've got time to figure things out."

She could see by his expression he wanted to argue with her, but to his credit, he nodded, and she could see her advice sinking in. She'd always loved that about West—that he had the rare ability to listen, when he wasn't barging forward with his agenda.

Soleil and West, having a baby together…by accident. It wasn't anything like the future she'd imagined for her son, but she could see the glimmers of a really beautiful life for them, if they could move past their differences long enough to let love take hold.

And Julia, for her part, would do whatever she could to help things along in the right direction.

CHAPTER FIVE

TWO DAYS HAD PASSED since she'd broken the news to West, and Soleil hadn't yet heard from him. The silence, frankly, was making her nervous. Was he just taking his time absorbing the news, or was he preparing to launch an attack on her life, some kind of conquer-and-occupy scenario? The longer he went without contacting her, the more she believed the latter. Did she really have the fortitude to stand up to him in a win-at-all-costs battle?

Thank goodness she only had two more days until her current batch of kids would go home, and the farm would shut down for winter break. She could hardly wait. Usually she hated to see them leave, but, with everything else going on, keeping up with them, overseeing their work and refereeing their battles all seemed to require too much of her limited stamina.

Soleil sat down at the computer, opened her Web browser and logged into her e-mail account. She was exhausted, and she hoped like crazy that she wouldn't have any urgent business e-mail waiting to be dealt with.

Twenty-two new messages appeared, about half of

which were junk. She set about deleting those, while scanning the subject lines of the relevant ones. One from her mother, ugh. One from the farm's development coordinator, which was likely urgent since it concerned a deadline for a grant they were applying for.

She opened it, scanned the message and decided it could wait until morning when she had a clearer head to write coherently.

Next she opened her mother's message with a sense of obligation. They hadn't been in contact for far too long. In fact, Soleil hadn't exactly gotten around to telling her mother she was pregnant, and now her guilt was growing by the day. There wasn't any simple way to explain away her silence. At least she'd sort of had an excuse with West.

Hi, Soleil,
Are you still alive? I haven't heard from you in ages. Did I mention my latest book will be out in two months? Will you be coming to visit for the holidays? I was hoping to spend a little time with you before I go on tour to promote the book. My publicist has four months' worth of readings and college speaking engagements lined up for me, and who knows if I'll survive.
Love, Mom

That was her mother's morbid sense of humor talking—amazing how she managed to work two death references into one casual e-mail. Former U.S. Poet Laureate Anne Bishop had never been known for her lightness of heart.

Soleil yawned and clicked Reply. Dealing with West over the holidays was about as much emotional turmoil as she could handle right now. She'd better let her mom know now that she was going to stay here for the Christmas festivities, so Anne could make alternate plans.

Hi, Mom,
Sorry you haven't heard from me. I've been busy and exhausted—which leads me to the news I have. I'm sorry to say I won't be visiting during the holidays. Maybe I'll make it down right after the new year, but for now I need the time to rest. I've had a particularly demanding group of kids this session. Congrats on the book release, by the way!
Love, S

There.

She was still unofficially the worst daughter in northern California for not telling her mom she was pregnant, but she'd have to sort that out after Christmas. For now, she was relieved to have one less holiday thing to think about.

Why *was* she so reluctant to tell people?

It was a question she'd been avoiding for months. Avoidance—her new hobby, apparently. And it went beyond any embarrassment in admitting she was

reneging in her I-don't-want-kids stance. As she
stared at the computer screen, at the long column of
e-mail messages she still needed to read and respond
to, the question wouldn't leave her alone.

Why?

The baby was going to arrive, regardless of
whether she told the people who needed to know. But
that wasn't an excuse.

The baby was going to arrive, and it was going to
transform her into someone new, just as her body was
being transformed now. She wasn't even sure if she
was going to like her new self. She certainly wasn't
all that crazy about her new, rotund body, with its
awkwardness and quickly shrinking mobility.

She feared her life was going to morph the same
way. She'd go from the ease of singledom to the diffi-
culty of single parenthood. And no one knew that dif-
ficulty better than her mother, even if she liked to claim
she'd had no problems raising her daughter alone.

Telling Anne, telling West, telling the world—it
amounted to admitting that she was about to give up
life as she knew it.

Although she'd never imagined herself being
happy about an unplanned pregnancy, in the moments
after she'd seen the plus sign appear on her home
pregnancy kit, Soleil had felt all sorts of unexpected
emotions. Bewilderment had given way to hope. She
hadn't been horrified. She'd been excited. She hadn't
been depressed. She'd been happy. And she'd known

without a moment's doubt that she wanted the baby. In that initial rush of excitement though, she'd failed to weigh all the consequences that had begun to weigh on her as the months passed and her changing body made her shifting reality more and more clear.

As much as she embraced the idea of having her baby, she was terrified of losing herself.

There. She'd admitted it. Not sure what to do with that fact, but she felt as if she could breathe a little easier now.

The sound of toenails clicking against wooden floors was a welcome distraction. She looked down to find Silas next to her, which reminded her of the thing she'd been promising herself she'd do with Tonio all day. She glanced at the clock—it was nine, so he'd still be awake.

The kids were expected to be in bed by ten, and after 9:00 p.m. was quiet reading time.

Soleil tugged gently on the dog's collar.

"Lie down," she commanded, and Silas did as she asked.

She stood. "Stay." The dog's muscles twitched, wanting to follow her. "No," she said. "Stay."

As she turned and left the room, he stayed still. His mournful gaze said he didn't like the situation, but he wasn't going to disobey.

She closed the door to the study—the coziest, most comforting room in the house—and went off in search of Tonio. She found him in the kitchen, getting himself a glass of water.

"Hey," she said, "I need to show you something in my office."

He took a long drink, put the glass down, then followed her out of the kitchen. When they reached the closed study door, he hesitated.

"What's in there?" he said.

It was time to work on his fear of dogs.

"My dog, Silas, is in there lying down. I'm going to go inside and hold on tight to his collar. I want you to come in and get used to being near him."

But Tonio was already shaking his head and backing away. "No way. I'm outta here."

She placed a hand on his arm. "Tonio. I won't make you do anything you don't want to do, okay? Do you believe me about that?"

He looked at her warily, his huge brown eyes half concealed by overgrown bangs that gave him a bit of a sheepdog look himself.

"An important thing to understand about dogs is that they can be trained to behave well. Silas is very well trained. As long as I've had him, he's never disobeyed me. If I tell him to stay, he'll stay. He won't come near you unless I allow him to."

He looked away and shrugged, trying hard to show that he didn't give a damn about her dog's obedience training.

"Were you hurt by a dog?" she asked.

His eyes flashed fear as he looked at her then looked away again. "Yeah," he half choked out.

"Will you tell me what happened?"

Silence.

She sighed. "You don't have to, but it might help."

More silence. But Soleil could be patient. Finally, standing her ground with the awkward silence paid off.

"I was little," he started, trying to appear cooler than he actually was. "Maybe four years old, and my family's dog attacked me one day when I got too near his food bowl while he was eating."

She let her hand slide down his arm to his hand, which she held tight, hoping he'd feel safe to keep talking.

"That must have been terrifying," she said when he went silent.

"I don't remember that much about it anymore. I remember it hurt a lot, and the dog's mouth…it looked so much scarier with blood on its muzzle. White fur, all stained with blood."

She could see from this distance in his gaze that he'd gone there mentally.

"How did you get away from the dog?"

"My mom found us and pulled him off me."

"Is that how you got the scar on your neck?"

He nodded. "I almost died from the attack."

Soleil frowned, unable to produce any adequate words.

"So now you see why I'm not going anywhere near that dog."

"I understand how terrified you are of dogs, and you have good reason to be."

He smirked, waiting for her *but*.

"It must be scary going through everyday life, when there are so many dogs around."

"Yeah, sometimes."

"When you applied to come here for the internship, did you see the part in the brochure about my dog?"

Tonio shrugged. "Yeah, but I figured... I don't know. I thought you'd keep him away from me."

"Maybe some part of you knew you needed to get used to having a dog around."

"Nuh-uh."

"An important part of this farm is Silas. He helps keep things running properly—and he's very unhappy when he doesn't have his job to do."

Tonio looked doubtful at this bit of information.

"It's true. And I want you to do me a favor."

"What?"

"I was a social worker before I started running this farm, and I've worked a few times with kids who've suffered from fear of dogs."

"Yeah, so?"

"I want you to trust me that I know how to help you be comfortable around dogs again."

"I don't want to be comfortable around dogs. It ain't like I'm getting me a pet pit bull or anything."

"No, but you do want to complete your internship, right?"

"The week's almost over, and I don't really care."

That, Soleil knew, was an outright lie. Judging by his application essay and his strong sense of right and wrong, Tonio was a community activist in the making. He'd be a great advocate for Urban Garden.

"Then why are you here?"

He shrugged again. "I thought it would be fun, but it's kind of lame."

She raised her eyebrows. "Fair enough, but as long as you're here, I'd like to help you get more comfortable around dogs."

He started shaking his head, but she said, "Do you trust me?"

"Sort of, I guess."

"I want you to spend five minutes with me in this room." She placed her hand on the closed door of the study.

"Why?"

"Because Silas is in there, and he's lying down, and he won't get up or even come near you unless I allow him to, and I won't, okay?"

"No way."

"Just five minutes, okay? I want to show you a few things about dogs that will help you in the future."

He sighed. "You promise he'll stay away from me?"

"Promise."

He stood there, resigned, waiting for her to open the door, so she did. Inside the room, Silas lay just where she'd left him, his tail wagging deliriously to see her again.

"Stay," she said again, and his tail slowed to a stop.

She went in ahead of Tonio and kept her body between him and the dog's. She crossed the room, sat next to Silas and took hold of his collar.

"Have a seat there on the sofa," she said to Tonio.

Nervously, he edged into the room, his gaze never leaving the dog's.

"While I'm holding on to Silas, I want you to come closer when you feel comfortable."

Tonio looked from her to the dog and back again. "If the dog's so obedient, why do you have to hold on to him?"

"I don't. He'll stay where he is until I tell him he can move, but I thought you might be more comfortable with me here holding him."

"This is stupid," he said. "Sitting here with a dog isn't going to make me like dogs again."

"I don't expect it to."

Instead of arguing further though, he stood and took a step closer, then another, then another. His movements were halting, and he seemed embarrassed to have her observing the whole thing.

"You're doing great," she said quietly. "Just kneel right here when you feel ready." She patted the ground next to her, a few feet from the dog.

Tonio dropped to his knees, then sat stiffly, staring at the dog with a look of absolute terror.

"You're okay," she said. "He's going to stay right where he is, and I'm going to have him roll onto his back."

"On your back," she said to Silas, loosening her grip on the collar, and he rolled.

The dog peered at them from his upside-down position, tongue lolling from the side of his mouth, paws bent in the air.

Tonio laughed a little. "He looks kinda silly like that."

Soleil rubbed the dog's belly and chest. "Yeah, he does. This is the dog's submissive posture. When he's like this, he can't hurt anyone, but others can hurt him."

"So that's why it's the submissive posture."

"Yep. When dogs meet each other, or sometimes when they meet people, and they want to show that they're trying to be friends, sometimes they'll flop onto their backs like this."

"Like their surrender flag?"

"They're telling the other dog that he or she is in charge."

Tonio watched the dog, a little more curious now than guarded. "I guess I've seen dogs do that."

"Dogs really care a lot about the social order. They need to know who is in charge all the time, and when they do, they're much happier, more well-behaved dogs."

"I don't think my brother's dog ever knew who was in charge."

"It's hard to know why he attacked you. But we can help you feel confident around dogs so that when you are with them, they know you're in charge."

"That doesn't mean they won't bite."

"No, you're right. But every dog and every situation is different. Let's consider this dog, right now. Do you think he's going to bite you?"

"He might."

"I've had him for six years, and he's never bitten anyone. It's not likely he'll do so now."

Tonio looked doubtful.

"Silas knows I'm the alpha dog here. I'm going to put my hand over his muzzle, and when I do, I'd like you to reach out and touch him."

"Hell, no."

"How about just on his tail?"

He half smiled. "This is still stupid."

She put her hand over Silas's mouth, and nodded at Tonio.

He reached out, slowly, slowly, and his hand grazed the very end of Silas's slowly thumping tail. As soon as he touched him and nothing happened, Tonio grew a bit bolder and moved his hand higher, to the dog's haunch. He gave Silas a tentative pat, then pulled his hand away, looking proud of himself.

Soleil smiled. "Great," she said. "You did great."

Tonio's gaze remained glued on the dog.

"I think that's enough progress for one day, don't you?" she continued.

He finally looked up at her with frightened puppy-dog eyes. "Can I go now?"

"Sure, but I want you to meet me again tomorrow, same time, same place. Deal?"

"Yeah, okay, whatever," he said as he hurried out of the room.

Soleil gave the dog a hard rub on his ears. "Good boy, Si."

She could relate to Tonio. His fear of dogs wasn't so different than her fear of West. Both of them had valid reasons for being afraid.

She put her hand on her belly, where a fluttering sensation had started, and she thought of West. He hadn't felt the baby's movements the way she had, hadn't had the time to let the reality of impending parenthood even settle on him yet. She'd really been a jerk to keep the truth from him for so long, and she felt horrible about it now.

She owed him the time to process his new reality and decide how he wanted to be involved. Even if the waiting was akin to torture.

CHAPTER SIX

FRIDAY AFTERNOON, Soleil was waving goodbye to her last batch of interns for the year. She still hadn't heard from West, and her anxiety was moving into the panicked range.

The last two days of camp had consumed her, but now the hubbub was over, and the farm was, thankfully, silent except for the sound of her assistant, Michelle, swaying on the porch swing nearby.

Back from her battle with the flu, she was beginning to look like a normal human again and had expressed a strong desire to get out and go for a walk today because she was so sick of being cooped up indoors.

"So," Soleil said, turning to Michelle. "Room service?"

The other woman rolled her eyes. *Room service* for them meant nothing in the way of luxury. Rather, it referred to the cleanup they had to do every time a group of interns left.

If they worked fast, they could get it done in a half hour and head for their favorite trail while there was still plenty of light.

"You're such a tyrant," Michelle complained, but she pushed herself off the swing and hurried inside. She liked to set an egg timer to see if they could beat their record time for getting the work done.

Soleil tried to forget her worries in the frenzy of cleaning, but as she was shoving laundry into the washer, she let her mind wander back to West. She realized with some horror that she was now even more disturbed by the prospect of him not caring about the baby at all than she was with the idea of having to fight off his well-intentioned advances.

God, she was screwed up.

Because the kids had done a pretty good job of cleaning up their rooms before leaving, Soleil and Michelle were finished in twenty minutes, and shortly thereafter, they were breathing in the fresh cold mountain air and working up a sweat as they hiked along the ridge overlooking the lake.

As they walked, Soleil filled Michelle in on the events of the days she'd missed. She desperately needed to talk to someone neutral about her West worries.

"You're lying," Michelle said in response to her biggest piece of news.

"I'm not," Soleil said, shaking her head, unable to contain a grin at her friend's shock.

"West Morgan did *not* just ride into town and nearly run over one of our goats."

"Why would I make that up?"

"Because you're cruel. Because you know this is exactly the kind of gossip I want to hear."

The path they followed went three miles on the high country trail at the top of the ridge overlooking Promise Lake. It was Soleil's favorite hike in the area, and it felt great to be getting some aerobic exercise finally.

"He saw that I was pregnant, of course, so I had to tell him."

"Oh, my God. You really are serious, aren't you?" Michelle was breathing heavily between words as they made their way up an incline in the trail, between a grove of pine trees and a poison oak–filled meadow.

"He completely freaked out."

Michelle stopped, forcing Soleil to stop, too.

"You did it! You finally told him. Oh, thank goodness."

Michelle had been oozing disapproval for weeks that Soleil was keeping the truth about the baby's father to herself. Michelle was, in fact, the only person who knew until three days ago when West had arrived.

"You don't have to make me sound so evil."

"You know that's not what I mean. It's just you don't need the stress of that confession hanging over your head. At least now things can move toward a resolution."

"*Things* don't need to move anywhere."

Michelle stopped staring at her and started walking again. "So what did he say?"

"Oh, the usual. 'How could you not have told me?' and 'Of course I'm going to be involved in this child's life.' Stuff like that."

"How can you be so flip about this? It's your child's father—and its future. *Your* future."

Her friend picked up her pace, possibly afraid of Soleil's foot making contact with her back end.

"God, could you chill out and trust that maybe I can handle my future without anyone else's help?"

"Okay, sorry." Michelle was silent for a moment, then she said, "He's going to want to marry you."

"Shut up."

"He is!"

"That's my worst nightmare."

"I know you say that, but…"

"But what?"

"You could do worse, you know."

"That's exactly what I hope to think about someone I pledge my life to—'I could do worse.'"

"West is gorgeous and smart and sexy and—"

"And you already know the hundred and one reasons I'm not interested in him."

"Let's see… Reason number one, he doesn't fit your fantasy of the perfect pseudo-hippie tree-hugging weenie?"

"I don't date *weenies,*" Soleil said, but it somehow rang false.

"Every guy you've ever dated has lived in a yurt or a commune or both and wouldn't hesitate to use the word *karma* in casual conversation."

"Except West."

"But you didn't really date, now, did you?" Michelle chided.

"I guess that depends on your definition of the word *date*."

"Alternately rolling around together naked and arguing doesn't really count in my book."

Soleil sighed. She'd never had such a volatile relationship with anyone before. Sure, she'd had her share of fireworks in the past, but with West it was an extended Fourth of July celebration—exhausting and explosive.

"That's the problem when you're with a guy with whom you agree about nothing."

"West seems a lot more reasonable to me than you make him out to be."

"He thinks women belong at home, barefoot and pregnant."

"You're halfway there, babe," Michelle said, clearly thrilled with her own joke.

"That's not funny."

"What exactly did he say? I mean, did he use the words *barefoot* and *pregnant*?"

"I don't remember, but that's what he meant." Even if he hadn't, Soleil refused to concede this point to Michelle. West's words conjured images of domestic prisons that easily fit the barefoot-and-pregnant mold.

Michelle shot her a pointed stare.

"I didn't memorize what he said word for word, okay?"

"Weren't you the one who told me once that you appreciated differences of opinion? That you would be bored to death by a guy who agreed with you about everything?"

"I don't think I said that."

"You did. You said it after your last breakup, actually."

Oh.

Right.

"That was a long time ago. Besides, Brian was so dull he would have made anyone long for a little excitement."

"And West excites you, right?"

"Not in a good way."

"Since when is there a bad kind of excitement?"

"Well, let's say you want to feel stable and secure and harmonious with your partner. Then excitement might not go hand in hand with that."

"Maybe you haven't given him enough of a chance yet. He seems like a great catch to me."

"Then *you* date him."

"I'm not the one about to have a baby with him."

"Yeah. There is that." Soleil looked out over the lake as they reached a scenic lookout spot.

To the southeast, she could see the farm, barely identifiable by its red rooftops at this distance. She'd come to love the place more intensely than anywhere else, and she wondered if she'd ever be able to love a man the way she loved her home. Certainly, she couldn't love West Morgan enough to give up this place for him.

"Don't you think if your baby has the chance to have both parents around watching him or her grow up, he or she deserves to have that?"

Ouch.

"You know, you're really laying it on thick today."

Michelle sighed. "Look, I know you have this vision of yourself as a strong woman who doesn't need anyone, but did it ever occur to you that you might feel differently once your baby is born?"

"I might, but I've got friends who can help me."

"You don't have any family here."

A weight settled on Soleil's chest. No, she didn't, and she didn't want to be reminded of that right now.

"Thank God," she said, trying to convince herself as much as Michelle. "If my mom was here, she wouldn't be any help anyway."

Which was true, but it would have been nice to have some kind of family around to help out.

Her face flushed, and she shrugged off her backpack and sat.

"Time for snacks," she said to distract from the fact that she was getting dizzy. "Can you imagine my mother playing the doting-grandma role?"

Michelle laughed. "She'd probably try to slip a little whiskey into the baby's bottle."

"Or write an angry poem about how demeaning it is to be called grandma."

Soleil took out two sandwiches and two bottles of water and began unwrapping her own turkey sandwich. Her hands were shaking from hunger, even though she'd had lunch a couple of hours earlier with the kids before they left. She took a big bite, and her shakiness began to subside.

"It's harder than it looks, raising a kid," Michelle said, still on her negativity kick. "Just remember that. Way harder."

Michelle's own daughter was eight years old, and while Soleil had been around for much of Kaitlin's childhood, she hadn't known their family for the first few years, before she'd moved to Promise and taken over the farm.

"I know I won't really understand what it's like until I'm in the middle of it. But I won't be the first person who's been a single parent. Look at my mom."

"Your father was there for the early years, though, right?"

"Yeah." It was only later, when her mother's depression and craziness went from bad to worse and she had an affair with a temporary resident scholar in the English Department at U.C. Berkeley that they split up.

Soleil had been six at the time. She remembered

it all only in a dreamlike way. And she remembered missing her father terribly, wanting him to
come back home.

She took a big bite of sandwich. Her own child
wouldn't miss what he or she had never known,
right? It would be different. For one thing, since
Soleil worked for herself, she could be around all the
time. Even if she had to hire a nanny part-time, she'd
never be farther than a quick jog away from the baby.

Michelle took off her jacket and spread it on the
ground, then sat and twisted her long dark hair up
into a bun.

"I'll be around to help, but honestly, Soleil, I don't
know how I would have survived the baby years with
Kaitlin without Daniel to help me."

"So divorce Daniel and marry me. We can make
the lesbian thing work, can't we?"

Michelle gave her a look. "Maybe you can, but
men have certain…qualities…that I can't do without."

"Oh, sure, rub it in that you've got certain *quali-
ties* to keep you entertained in bed at night while I'm
all alone."

"By choice," Michelle reminded her.

"The weird thing is, I thought I'd be hearing from
West again right away. And I haven't."

"You freaked him out, of course. Can you imagine having someone tell you out of the blue that
you're about to have a baby? Talk about the shock
of a lifetime."

Something else was nagging at her. West wouldn't be back in town at this time of year unless something was wrong. She hadn't even bothered to ask what that might be.

She should call him, she decided. Invite him to go to her next ultrasound appointment on Monday.

That would kind of, sort of, make up for a few things, wouldn't it?

Maybe not, but it was a start.

WEST STOOD in the doorway and looked across the floor of his father's kitchen, where a river of milk meandered across the tile, curving its way past islands of oat-bran cereal.

"Dad, what happened?"

"Huh? Oh, that." His father edged past him into the kitchen. "Somebody's damn cat tripped me."

"Where is the cat?"

"I locked the ornery thing outside where it belongs. Don't know what it was doing in here in the first place. Is it yours?"

"Yes, he's mine," West lied, hoping it would keep the cat safe for the time being. They'd been going around and around about Moe the cat for the past few days. It was crazy-making how conversations they'd had minutes earlier would resurface, again and again and again and again, ad infinitum.

"I'd appreciate it if you'd let him stay inside when it's cold out."

"I never did like cats," the General grumbled as he peered in the refrigerator.

Entirely untrue. His dad had adored Moe.

Had? The word sent a chill up West's spine. He'd begun to think of his father as if he was already gone, as if this belligerent man a few feet away wasn't actually the General.

He was, but he wasn't. All the things that had made him who he was were fading fast, leaving behind a person West barely recognized. His father had once been a passionate duck hunter, a fisherman, an avid golfer, a reader of historical biographies, a lover of talk radio and a dispenser of unwanted advice. He'd been a doting cat lover who spoiled Moe with fresh fish and frequent brushings. He'd been pushy and pigheaded and arrogant, always. But he'd also been a man of unwavering moral fortitude. There had never been an ounce of doubt in West's mind that his dad tried his best to do the right thing.

And now… How could he have lost the essence of himself? Where had his dad gone?

West grabbed a handful of paper towels from the counter and began cleaning up the mess on the floor. Thank God his father hadn't tripped over the cat, or slipped in the milk and suffered a fall.

He'd gotten the cereal and milk halfway cleaned up when he heard the doorbell ring. His father ignored the sound, so West stood and went to the front door, wet paper towels still in hand.

He found his mother standing on the front porch. She gave him a grim look.

"What's wrong, Mom? What are you doing here?"

"Oh, nothing's wrong," she said. "It's just odd being here again…" She was looking around as if seeing everything for the first time. "I don't think I've come back to the house since the divorce."

He absorbed this information. And it was true— it was odd having his mother standing on the porch of the last home where they'd been a family. She should have fit right in here, but she didn't anymore, not when she looked so whole and healthy and set apart from the decay that had overtaken the place.

"Did you come here to see me?"

"I came to see you and your father both."

West was stunned silent. His parents hadn't exactly had an amicable divorce, thanks mostly to his father's unwavering insistence that he was right and Julia was wrong about everything. As a result they didn't stop by for impromptu visits with each other.

"I've thought about your dilemma, and I've decided to help with your father's care."

His silence grew louder, and he realized his mouth was hanging open.

"I know this is unexpected," she said calmly. "But it's what my conscience is telling me to do."

"But… Mom, I don't know. Things are difficult here."

"I'm better equipped to deal with him than most people are."

"You got divorced for good reasons." West shook his head, trying to absorb this new, bizarre turn of events.

Maybe his mother was losing her marbles, too. But standing there in her red wool coat and with her gray hair perfectly neat and her brown eyes so warm and alert, he couldn't see the slightest hint of craziness.

And he was relieved to see her. She was capable. She'd know what to do.

"I don't expect you to understand now, but you will someday, once you've been married to someone for a good portion of your life."

She said this with such finality, West knew better than to argue. His mother didn't make any decision rashly. She'd probably been up all night thinking about it.

But this…

This didn't sound like his mom talking.

"What do you mean by *help?*" he finally asked.

"I mean, I'm volunteering to be his primary-care person until he needs more intensive care than I can provide."

"I don't know if that's a good idea. He'll drive you crazy," West said, his voice lowered so that his father couldn't overhear.

"You said he's been sexually harassing his caregivers, right?"

West nodded, not all that inclined to discuss the matter further with his mother.

"I'm the one woman he's sure not to sexually harass," she said as if that decided the matter.

Okay, so maybe she just needed to see for herself what she was getting into.

"Mom…"

"Don't argue with me. My mind is made up."

He was silent, trying to decide what he could say.

"West, please, don't make this any more difficult than it already is."

"If you're sure about this…"

"I am."

"Come on in and have a visit with your new patient then."

Her expression grew the faintest bit uncertain. "Will he recognize me, do you think?"

"Yeah, I think he will," West said, though he didn't know anything about his dad for sure these days. "I'll get you a cup of coffee, and you can say hi to him."

He stepped aside and motioned her in.

His mother looked even more apprehensive now, but she took a tentative step forward, then another, until she was all the way inside.

She looked around at what had changed and what had stayed the same. He recalled how the foyer used to be filled with the scent of fresh flowers, where now there was only a stale odor of last night's dinner mingled with the faint scent of cat pee.

To their right, the formal living room looked nothing like it used to, West recalled. It had gone through the decorating changes of two wives, along with his father's own sparse tendencies. Where once there had been family photos on the mantel, now there was nothing but an antique clock because his father didn't see the point of having so many "dust catchers" sitting around.

To the left the study, which had always been his father's domain, had barely changed in all the years he'd owned the house. Same imposing desk, same shelves of books, same military awards and prints covering the walls, same air of severity that had always dominated his father's life...until recently.

"He's in the kitchen," West said, leading his mom down the hallway, toward the sound of his father muttering.

"Was that his cat I saw on the front lawn?"

"Yeah, he's banished from the house right now because Dad doesn't remember having a cat," West whispered.

His mother's expression turned even darker. "I'll be sure and pick up some allergy medicine today," she said, her light tone sounding forced.

"Who's there?" his father called as they entered the kitchen.

West held out a hand to keep his mom from stepping in the spilled cereal.

"Dad, it's Mom. She stopped in to say hi."

His father turned, scowling, toward them. "Julia, where the hell have you been?" he demanded, as if she'd stepped out for groceries and had stayed gone for ten years.

She looked from the General to West, bewildered, but she answered, "Oh, here and there. How have you been, John?"

"Awful," he muttered, taking out a pan now and putting it on the stove.

He cranked up the knob on the front of the stove and a flame burst up around the pan.

"Hey, Dad, why don't you let me do that." West made a move for the knob to turn it down, but his father waved him away.

"Leave me the hell alone and let me cook my own eggs." He turned down the flame, put a pat of butter in the pan and fumbled with the egg carton on the counter.

West looked over at his mother, and they winced at each other.

"I remember how much you loved my omelets," Julia said. "Sure you wouldn't like me to whip one up for you?"

For the first time since West had been back home, his father smiled.

"Now that you mention it, that sounds perfect."

She went to the refrigerator and brought out the mushrooms and cheddar cheese West had bought yesterday. West sat and watched a disconcerting time warp occur right in front of him.

All of a sudden, he was transported back over a decade and a half. His parents hadn't divorced. They'd just aged. Two more marriages and years of bitterness didn't lie between them.

His father, for the first time in ages, looked sort of…content.

It was heartbreaking.

And he wondered if any woman would ever love him enough to show up and take care of him when he'd become too impossible to care for. Or vice versa.

Could he love Soleil this way?

Or was this even love he was witnessing?

It resembled it, but it also resembled something his parents were far more familiar with: duty.

And right now, he wasn't so sure there was much difference between the two.

He hadn't gotten in touch with Soleil since she'd told him about the baby, partly because he was terrified, and partly because he was trying to take his mother's advice and give the matter time and space, take things slowly, try not to force a resolution.

Everything in him wanted to force a resolution, and he knew if he called Soleil, he'd find it nearly impossible not to start steering the situation in the right direction. Marriage, harmony, family.

Leaving it alone hadn't been so hard, thanks to his father, who'd kept him busy. Margie, the temporary attendant, had bailed yesterday when his father had groped her then an hour later tried to hit her for attempting to help him in the bathroom.

And now here was his mother, the latest candidate for the attendant job, and by far the most experienced.

Did the idea make sense, or was it crazy?

"So, has West told you his big news?" she asked the General, interrupting West's brooding.

Oh, God.

What was she thinking? Of course he hadn't told his dad.

"What? What's she talking about?" His father gave him a confused look.

"Oh, actually, I haven't mentioned it yet." He gave his mother a little glare when she glanced at him from the stove, and she raised her eyebrows in silent reproach.

"Well?" she nudged. "I think he deserves to hear the good news."

"Dad, my, um, girlfriend and I are going to be having a baby in May."

"What girlfriend?"

"You haven't met her. I'll have to introduce you soon."

"You got some girl pregnant, and you're not even married? Who is this girl? Why the hell haven't I met her yet?" His father banged his fist on the kitchen table to punctuate the rant.

"I don't really want to get into it right now, Dad. I'll introduce you soon."

"Since when is it okay for an air force officer to go around having babies out of wedlock? In my day, an officer didn't do that kind of thing."

"I know, Dad. But things happen. Soleil and I haven't worked out how we're going to handle things."

"What the hell's a *So-lay?*"

"Soleil is my girlfriend's name. It's a French word. It means sun."

His father still looked perplexed, then, predictably, angry. "What is she, some kind of hippie?"

West ignored that. He glanced at his mom, whose expression was worried now. She turned her gaze from West to the omelet she was watching in the pan. She knew better than to jump into the middle of things.

"You mean to tell me, you got some girl pregnant, and you're not even marrying her?" He slammed his fist on the table again, causing the salt and pepper shakers to jump this time. "What kind of man are you, anyway? You're not a man I raised, that's for damn sure."

Before West could react, his father pushed himself to his feet and walked out of the room, down the hall to his study. It wouldn't do any good to follow him, so West simply let out a ragged breath.

"Mom," he said. "Why…"

He didn't even have the energy to say the question out loud. But she knew what he wanted to know— why'd she have to go and tell the General?

"Better to get it out in the open now, rather than later. It would only get harder to explain."

"You could have let me do it in my own time."

She eased the omelet off the hot pan and onto a plate. "West, dear, I'm sorry. I think I saved you some trouble, though. If you'd tried to tell him on your own, he'd have been worse. With me here as a buffer—"

"Yeah, okay, you're right."

And she was. Since childhood, her presence had been the buffer between himself and his father. When she was near, the General was slightly less hostile, slightly more tolerable. Some things never changed, apparently.

As he watched his mother carry the plate to the study, he recognized he definitely didn't belong here. He didn't want to be in the middle of this family drama anymore.

Maybe his mother was crazy, too, showing up out of the blue, whipping up an omelet as if she'd never left the place—a mad Betty Crocker bent on reconciliation. Had loneliness finally gotten to her? Was this the first sign of her own mental decay?

He craved an escape from this place. He was tired of trying to please his father, and he wasn't going to do it anymore.

What that would mean, though, he couldn't say.

CHAPTER SEVEN

SOLEIL COULDN'T KEEP excluding West. She'd avoided the inevitable all weekend, taking long naps and wrapping up loose ends around the farm's operation and finances before the end of the year. Today was going to be the first day she did things right.

She found his number in her cell-phone address book and hit the Call button. A moment later, his voice was on the other end of the line, sounding clear, as if he'd already been up for a while.

"West," she said tentatively. "I know it's early, but I'm calling because I have an ultrasound appointment today, and I thought you might like to join me for it."

Silence.

"I mean, you know, because you'd get to see the baby on the ultrasound screen."

"Oh, um…of course," he finally said, sounding strange. "I'd love to go. What time?"

"It's at noon in Santa Rosa. Sorry for the short notice."

"So, an hour to get there…" A pause. "I'll pick you up at ten-thirty, if that works for you."

She blinked, stunned. "Uh, sure. That would be great."

"I'll see you in two hours then."

She hung up. In two hours, she'd be driving to the city with West, just like a real couple on their way to see their real baby on an ultrasound screen.

Maybe he'd also want to join her for her Bradley childbirth classes at the community center. Of course he would, and he'd have some definite ideas about what to name the baby—something traditional like Elizabeth or Michael, or maybe even after his own parents...

She had always dreamed of having a normal name that people could spell, instead of the bizarre hippie name her mother had actually chosen. As a girl, she'd dreamed of being a Melissa or a Jennifer. Probably the kind of name West would like.

Okay, stop. You need to calm down and get a grip. Quit getting so far ahead of yourself.

The two hours zipped by as she got ready, answered a few phone calls and made a list of things she needed to buy. Most important, she needed to find a crib. Her father had sent her a check—his way of apologizing for being at a conference in Europe instead of any-where accessible for the holidays—and intended to use that money to start outfitting the nursery.

When she finally heard West's car in the gravel driveway outside, she was seized by a moment of ter-ror. This wasn't just any trip to the doctor they were embarking on. This was something huge. This was the thing Soleil had been avoiding ever since she'd first learned she was pregnant.

She'd been lying to herself all this time, convinced that somehow the pregnancy, and the baby, belonged to her alone. Now she had to face the truth—West was going to be a big part of her life from here on out, whether she liked it or not.

She heard the vehicle stop out front and a door shut. She barely had time to check herself in the mirror before hurrying out the door. West was a few feet from the SUV.

He smiled and said hello.

"I could drive if you want," she said.

He patted the hood of the Toyota Highlander. "Great gas mileage. I'll drive."

He opened the passenger door for her. She climbed in, then dug a package of saltines out of her purse for emergency motion-sickness use.

"Cracker?" She offered the package to West as he got in the driver's side.

"No, thanks. You still get morning sickness?"

"No, but I do get carsick sometimes. I probably won't, but crackers seem to head it off at the pass."

He drove toward the main road. "So have you seen an ultrasound of the baby before?"

"Once, at twelve weeks. It looked like a tiny alien with a heartbeat."

"Do they give you a photo or anything to keep?"

"Sure," she said. "I bet they'll give a copy to each of us."

Their baby now. Not hers alone, but *theirs*.

She watched him sideways, a little surprised how quickly he'd gone from shock and awe to asking for baby pictures.

"So…um, do we get to find out the sex of the baby?"

"If we want to."

"*Do* we want to?"

We?

Do we *want to?*

She popped a cracker into her mouth and chewed furiously as her freak-out quotient shot through the roof of the vehicle.

"I'm not really sure what I want to do. I mean, a surprise is fun, I guess, but part of me is dying to know."

"Okay, well, it's up to you. I'll go with whatever you want."

Awfully diplomatic of him.

"Have you thought about names at all?" he asked.

Soleil recalled her earlier fear about his naming preferences and popped a second cracker in her mouth. Why hadn't she thought to bring some seltzer water, too?

"I have a few ideas."

He glanced over at her. "Care to share them?"

"Maybe later. I'm feeling a little carsick right now."

"Should I pull over?"

"No, no, that's okay. The crackers are helping."

"If it's a girl, I've always liked my mom's name, Julia."

Of course he did.

She tried not to visibly wince at how right her fears had been. West was doing exactly what she thought he'd do—barging right in and taking over the whole baby-preparation process as if gearing up for battle. Leaving no detail to chance.

Julia was a lovely name. And a lovely woman. But Soleil wasn't exactly ready to have this kind of lovey-dovey-couple discussion with a man she didn't love.

"Not that I'm saying we should use that name. I really haven't ever thought about what I'd name a kid, frankly."

"Okay," she said with another stab of guilt over her lateness in telling him he was about to be a father.

"How about your mom? What's her name?"

"*My* mom?"

Naming a baby girl after Soleil's mother wouldn't be so different from naming her after a barracuda.

"Anne," she finally said. "Her name is Anne."

"You know, you've never told me about your mother, or any of your family."

Yeah, it hadn't exactly come up when they were sweating and rolling around in bed together.

Ahead, the road curved through a valley between pale yellow hills that bulged like pregnant bellies against the horizon. The sky had mercifully turned blue again today, a clear crystalline blue that promised warm weather. So much easier to focus on than the circumstances of her life.

"Hello? Don't want to talk about your family?"

"Not really," she said, staring at a herd of cattle on a distant hillside.

"I understand. But it might be weird if I don't know anything about my own kid's grandparents."

"Anne Bishop," Soleil said. "That's my mom. She's a poet."

"Wait, you mean like *the* Anne Bishop? The one I had to study in college?"

"That would be her."

"Wow. I didn't realize."

"When I went to school at Berkeley, there was a whole class devoted to her work."

"Did you take it?"

"Hell, no."

"Are you close to her?"

"Close…isn't exactly what I'd call us. I mean, we tend to butt heads a lot. We're frighteningly similar people, both way too headstrong and stubborn."

"You? Headstrong and stubborn? No way." His wry smile betrayed his earnest tone, and Soleil chuckled.

"I know it's hard to believe."

"What about your father? Were your parents married?"

"My dad is a civil-rights attorney. My mom cheated on him when I was a kid, and they split up.

But they were so different, I don't think they'd have survived even without the affair."

"Different how?"

Soleil laughed at the absurdity of her parents together. "My dad was a Black Panther for a while in the seventies. Having a white wife didn't exactly fit with his radical leanings back then."

"Oh."

"Oddly enough, my parents gave me plenty of reason to swear off interracial relationships."

West's eyebrows shot up. "I don't understand… If you're half black and half white, which race are you swearing off?"

She couldn't help but laugh. "Touché. My experience going through the world with light brown skin is, people tend to classify me as black, African-American, whatever you want to call me, and that's how I identify myself."

"I guess that makes sense."

"No, it doesn't totally make sense, but it's the way the world works."

And the one time she broke her own rule and let herself fall hard, she'd gotten her heart shattered by a guy who didn't have the balls to defy his assbackward white family and stay with her.

"So where does that leave us?"

She shrugged. "I guess the universe has a few lessons to teach me about how we're all a rainbow of people or some crap like that."

"Are you close to your father at all?"

"Sadly, no. He moved to Chicago after the split. He's the type who lives and breathes his work. So it's hard to develop the distance father-daughter thing."

"Sorry to hear that."

"It's okay. If he'd stuck around, my mom probably would have killed him. So he saved her a prison sentence. He's a good guy, if absorbed in his life."

Soleil's motion sickness hadn't completely disappeared, so she fixed her eyes forward on the horizon as she ate another cracker.

She normally reserved discussing the family for guys she was really serious about…which was why she'd never talked to West about her parents before. And yet, whether she'd intended to be serious about him or not, they were on their way to see their baby together for the first time.

Just like a real couple.

Wasn't this about as real as it got?

The truth of their situation struck Soleil again, and a cold sweat broke out on her face. She dug another cracker out of the package and ate it as if it would save her life.

WEST TOOK ONE LOOK around the waiting room of the doctor's office and swallowed hard. Pink walls decorated with black-and-white photos of naked babies surrounded them. He fit in this place about as well as a foot fit into a glove.

Three pregnant women besides Soleil occupied the chairs, each one looking more ready to pop than the next. A tired-looking woman with a brand-new baby—so new it was still kind of red and wrinkled—sat closest to the door. The baby was in one of those big plastic car-seat things that had a handle, making the baby more convenient to carry around, apparently.

West was the only guy in the room—possibly the only guy in the entire building—and the estrogen in the air was enough to make him want to go do something manly like check under the hood of his car, or maybe hunt for wild boar.

While Soleil checked in at the front desk, he zeroed in on the magazine selection and tried to find something to distract himself. *Parenting, Baby, Woman's Day, Fit Pregnancy*…a far cry from the waiting rooms on the air force base, where *Soldier of Fortune* and *Sports Illustrated* dominated the tabletop selections. So he decided to embrace the femininity and grabbed the latest issue of *Baby*.

He sat and was about to start flipping through the magazine when Soleil put down her purse next to him.

"I'll be right back," she said, holding up a little plastic cup and wincing.

"Where's my cup?" he joked, and she rolled her eyes before disappearing through a doorway.

As West watched her walk away, something unexpected stirred in him. The way Soleil walked said everything about her. She knew who she was and where she was going. She was comfortable in her skin, and even as her body changed with pregnancy, her walk maintained that signature confident, sexy stride he'd found so attractive in the summer.

Some part of him still wanted her.

It wasn't the time to be thinking that way. Not yet, anyway. He needed a distraction, so he turned his attention back to the periodical.

The first article he encountered was "Ten Painful Breast-feeding Problems Solved!" and if it hadn't been for the buxom breast barely concealed by a baby's head covering the page facing the article, he would have moved on to something else. Instead, he lingered and learned all about what "latching on" meant and how important it was to make sure the baby was doing it properly.

By the time Soleil returned, cup free, he'd also learned about engorgement—*ouch!*—and mastitis.

She read over his shoulder.

"You'll be relieved to know," she whispered after a moment, "you won't actually have to do that. It's mostly the mom's job."

"I just want to be educated in case you come to me with complaints about your chafed nipples."

He started to read the next article, "What Your Baby Is Telling You Without Saying a Word."

Beside him, Soleil produced an issue of the *New Yorker* from her purse, apparently disinterested in the unspoken language of babies.

He glanced over her shoulder and caught her chuckling at a David Sedaris essay.

"That's not going to teach you anything you need to know about babies," he whispered, only half joking.

She looked at him as if he was crazy. "Just because I'm having a baby doesn't mean I have to turn into a boring dolt who thinks and talks about nothing but my child."

Part of him took offense at her tone and wanted to bring her down a notch. "Do you know what to do when your milk duct gets clogged?"

"No, but I'm sure you'll be right there to tell me."

West resisted making any more inflammatory comments, because Soleil suggesting that he might be around to tell her such things was progress enough for one day. No need to push his luck.

But, was that what he actually wanted? To be around, giving her breast-feeding pointers?

A day ago, he'd never given a moment's thought to the complications faced by nursing mothers, and today he was claiming to be educated on the subject.

Was this who he was becoming?

West had always thought of himself first and foremost as an air force Special Forces officer. He lived for his work. He'd always thought of it as who he was, as well as what he did.

But it was only his job. It was something he did for a living. He was also a guy who loved rock climbing, camping, backcountry hiking, kayaking and distance running. Of course that was all more stuff he did. It wasn't really him, was it?

Becoming a father though—that felt like a change in the core of his very being. It wasn't something he could pick up for a while, like tennis, and discard when he tired of it.

For the rest of his life, no matter what else changed, he would always be a father.

As he stared at the magazine on his lap, his vision went blurry for a few moments. He focused on an article about how to make organic baby food. He closed the magazine and looked around. The women who'd been here when they'd arrived had all been called in without his noticing it. Across from them, another couple was just sitting down.

The guy caught his eye. The same deer-in-headlights expression that West was sure he wore was faintly visible on the other man's face. West smiled and nodded, and the man nodded back, then looked at the selection of magazines and opted to sit and stare at the wall.

West watched the other couple, who were whispering to each other now. They were far enough away that he couldn't hear what they were saying, but he could tell by their body language and gestures that they were in love.

The man placed a hand on his wife's huge belly, on a spot she indicated, and smiled at her. He must have been feeling the baby kick.

Had Soleil felt their own baby kick?

He wouldn't know.

How did they look to others? Each of them sitting stiffly, not touching, not talking, they must have looked as if they were waiting for grim news.

He didn't want it to be like this. Okay, he'd never imagined how it would be to await a baby's arrival, and he'd never imagined getting a woman pregnant by accident. But now they were in this predicament, so it was time to figure out how he wanted circumstances to unfold.

Soleil giggled again at the article she was reading.

"Mind reading it to me?" West dared to ask. "I think I've learned all I need to know about breast-feeding for now."

"Hold on," she said, not even looking up. "I'm almost done. You can read it yourself."

How were they supposed to make the best of it when she shot him down at every turn?

The door to the examining rooms opened, and a nurse called, "Soleil Freeman?"

West looked at Soleil. "Come on back with me," she said, so he stood and followed her through the door and down the hallway to the room the nurse indicated they enter.

"You can change into the gown behind the curtain," she said. "When you're ready, pull back the curtain and the doctor will be in to see you shortly."

West took a seat in a pink plastic chair against a lavender wall. Was there anything in this place that wasn't designed to look girlie?

On the wall next to him was a bulletin board filled with pictures of new babies, some alone and some in the arms of grinning parents. A few lay in cribs with siblings standing next to them or propped on the laps of awkward-looking children who clearly had never held a baby before.

Soleil stepped behind the curtain and drew it as the nurse closed the door.

"No peeking," she said, only half joking, he suspected.

"I've already seen you naked, you know."

"Trust me, I've got a daily reminder."

He heard her shuffling as she disrobed, and he tried to imagine how her body had transformed in pregnancy. Fuller breasts, rounder curves... She'd once had a waist so small he could put his hands around it and nearly touch fingers on both sides.

He shifted in his seat, aroused by his train of thought. Turning his attention back to the photos on the wall, he found instant relief.

Soleil pulled back the curtain to reveal an examining table with some complicated-looking equipment and a video screen next to it. She was wearing a hospital gown—pink, of course—and gave him a look that made it clear she didn't need any cute comments about her attire.

The doctor knocked, then came in and introduced herself as Dr. Singh.

"This is West, the baby's father," Soleil said by way of introduction.

West smiled. "Nice to meet you."

"Likewise," the doctor said. She turned to Soleil. "Do you have any questions or concerns before we get started?"

"I've been getting eczema lately. Do you think that could be related to the pregnancy?" Soleil asked.

West was too nervous now to pay close attention to the answer. He watched Soleil, who was both familiar and foreign to him, and he wondered again about the strange twists of fate that had brought them here together today.

Deep down, something tugged at him. He recalled the laughter they'd shared last summer, the passion, the carefree way they'd come together for two short weeks—some of the best times of his life.

Did Soleil feel the same? If she did, she'd never admit it. She was more disturbed by their differences than he had been. She was the one with the temper he'd so enjoyed toying with. She took him seriously, which was both charming and a source of endless strife.

But he'd enjoyed their fights, too. He loved watching her tense for battle. When she was angry, her green eyes glowed as if a fire burned inside her, and she could hurl an insult like no one else he'd ever met. The freedom of saying exactly what they felt— no dancing around anyone's feelings—was one of the most liberating sensations he'd ever experienced in a relationship.

Soleil, on the other hand, had merely found him infuriating.

Dr. Singh went through the motions of a routine exam, then she asked Soleil to lie back on the table. She squeezed a bunch of clear jelly on Soleil's stomach and began poking around with an ultrasound wand.

"Come closer," she said to West, "so you can see."

He stood and went to Soleil's side. Before he could brace himself for the shock, a blurry image appeared on the video screen. Dr. Singh pointed to one end of the blob.

"That's your baby's head…and there's the heart, the spine, the arms, the feet…"

West's mouth went dry, and everything he thought he knew and felt was suddenly turned upside down.

There was his baby.

There was *their* baby.

A wave of dizziness hit him, and he sat on the edge of the examining table to steady himself.

Their baby.

He could see the baby's too-big head, and its delicate limbs curled up like a spring bud waiting to bloom. He could see the tiny spine, and the *blip-blip* of a heart pumping.

His own heart stopped for a beat.

He looked at Soleil, and she was smiling in a way he'd never seen her smile before. She glowed like a child on Christmas morning who'd gotten her heart's desire.

This was not the Soleil he knew. This was a glimpse of someone new.

She caught his eye, and for a moment they were looking at each other instead of the baby. Then they both looked back at the video screen.

"Would you like to know the baby's gender?" the doctor asked.

West and Soleil looked at each other again, and simultaneously they said, "Yes."

"You're going to have a little girl. Congratulations."

The sheer joy that he'd seen a moment earlier in Soleil's expression was replaced by something else entirely. Something like amazement.

He was sure it matched his own expression.

"Really?" West said. "A girl? You're sure?"

"As sure as I can be," the doctor said as she moved the ultrasound wand around on Soleil's belly.

She was attempting to get a better image of the baby's bottom half.

"Let's see if I can get her to shift a bit, so we can make sure nothing's hiding behind the umbilical cord."

"It's a girl," Soleil said, sounding certain. "I've been thinking it was a girl since the moment I knew I was pregnant."

The doctor smiled as she continued to watch the screen. "Never argue with a mother's intuition." She held the wand still. "See there?"

She was indicating an area of the screen that just looked like a bunch of blurry nothing to West.

"I think we can rest assured you'll be having a little girl in a few more months. Would you like a picture of her?"

"Could you make a copy for each of us?" Soleil asked.

"Certainly." Dr. Singh typed something on the computer keyboard. "You can pick up your prints from the nurse at the front desk."

She used a mouse to measure the baby's head circumference and length, then added, "And judging by the baby's size, I'd say your due date of May 1 is right on."

May 1.

He'd somehow neglected to ask Soleil about the exact due date.

May 1 was the day he'd hold his little girl for the first time. She would no longer be a possibility—she'd be an actuality, a real live person whose life he was responsible for.

Soleil caught his eye. Her gaze searched him for the answer to some question she hadn't asked. Maybe she wanted to see how he felt.

How *did* he feel?

Overwhelmed, terrified, thrilled, overjoyed, sick to his stomach and as shaky as a drunk without his booze.

She must not have liked what she saw in his eyes, because her expression darkened, and she shifted her focus to the ultrasound screen, which was now blank.

Dr. Singh was wiping away the gel she'd put on Soleil's belly with a cloth. "Everything looks to be progressing fine. Do you have any questions?"

Lots. Such as, how was he supposed to be a good father? And, why did babies have to happen by accident like this? And, how badly damaged would his daughter be if her mother and father couldn't get along?

He shrugged and gave Soleil a questioning look.

"None for me," she said. "When is the next ultrasound?"

"Unless something unusual comes up, we may not need to do another."

"Okay. I was thinking for West, but—" she seemed to realize too late that she'd touched upon a controversial subject, and her voice faltered "—you'll be gone again."

She busied herself with sitting up and rearranging

the gown, while West absorbed the truth. He would be gone. He'd be back in Colorado, or wherever his next assignment took him, and she'd be here. At least he presumed she planned to be here. And why wouldn't she, when her life and everything she loved was wrapped up in the farm?

"Oh? Where do you live?" Dr. Singh asked, confused now.

"I'm in the air force, stationed in Colorado at the moment but waiting for my next assignment." Which could take him anywhere, at any time, with little notice.

He caught the tightening of Soleil's expression, and a deadweight settled on his chest. How had he been stupid enough to assume anything would be simple from this point forward?

A moment ago, he'd been imagining himself holding their newborn baby in his arms, when the reality was, he was far more likely to be thousands of miles away, cradling an assault rifle. He wouldn't even be present at his child's birth.

And it was no wonder Soleil was reluctant to depend on him for anything.

"So, you're…" Dr. Singh said, trying to piece together the situation, "not planning to be together?"

"No," Soleil said, her tone final.

West felt the word like a punch in the gut, although it shouldn't have surprised him. It was exactly what he'd have expected her to say, wasn't it?

"We're still trying to work out how we'll share parenting duties," he said.

"I see." the doctor said. "Well, I hope to see you again," she said to West as she went to the door.

To Soleil she said, "I'll see you next month."

"I'll go out to the desk and get our pictures while you change," he told Soleil, and she nodded.

He needed to get away from her right now. The contrast between the high of seeing their baby for the first time and the low of getting slapped in the face with the truth was too much. He needed a chance to regroup before she nailed him with any more of her harsh reality.

In the safety of the waiting room, he asked the woman at the reception window for the ultrasound photos, and he felt a bit of the tension drain from his shoulders. As he gazed at an image of the baby, he almost couldn't bear the enormity of it. Tears came to his eyes, and he blinked stupidly.

Tears?

What the hell was happening to him? He wasn't the kind of guy who got choked up at the sentimental parts of movies, and he couldn't remember the last time he'd felt the sting of tears in his eyes.

He faked interest in something on the wall and forced his mind to go blank for a moment until he'd recovered. As he studied the framed print, he slowly allowed himself to consider what he needed to deal with next.

Soleil, their future, his career, hers, how to join their lives for the sake of the baby… Was it even possible?

It had to be. He had to be involved in his child's life. The alternative was unimaginable. And yet, he couldn't quite imagine how to make it happen, either.

That was why he and Soleil needed to talk.

In that brief moment of hopefulness, when they'd seen their baby together on the ultrasound screen, he'd felt a powerful connection to Soleil. That connection was evidenced by the photos in his hand. He had to hold on to that feeling of hope, because there had to be some way they could make a family.

CHAPTER EIGHT

SOLEIL HAD NEVER GAZED longingly at other people's babies, wishing for one of her own. She liked babies well enough, enjoyed holding them, thought they were cute and all. But ached for one?

Not at all.

So when she saw her own child's ultrasound image, looking so much more like a real baby than it had at twelve weeks, she was surprised at the overwhelming ache, coming from somewhere so deep down she couldn't begin to pinpoint its origin.

Even after they'd left the doctor's office, she could still feel its grip on her, almost choking in its intensity.

West, for his part, looked shell-shocked yet again. She wondered if he was feeling as freaked out as she was, but she wasn't ready to talk about it.

That look on his face during the ultrasound—it had spoken volumes. She'd seen in his eyes the same wonder she'd been feeling, and she'd understood in that moment that the baby was as big a deal for him as it was for her.

Of course, he didn't have to watch his body taken

over by it, and his life wouldn't change in the same ways hers would, but he was, no doubt, profoundly affected.

Remorse like she'd never felt before crept up on her as they walked across the parking lot. What had she done? What on earth had she been thinking, not telling him about the pregnancy from the start? Now things were such a tangled mess. They had so far to go, so much to sort out before they could begin to see the way toward a resolution.

But what if…

Maybe…

The hope she'd felt while looking at their baby's image minutes ago dared a resurgence. West was here. And she was here. They were two caring adults. Somehow, they could make this work, couldn't they?

Back in the car, she dug around in her purse for more crackers and found instead a voice-mail notice on her cell phone. Grateful for the distraction, she checked the message.

It was her mom, saying that she'd decided to come to stay for the holidays, that she'd be arriving tomorrow.

Tomorrow?

"Oh, God," Soleil muttered into the phone as West settled in the driver's seat.

"What's wrong?"

She deleted the message and put her phone away. "It's my mother. She's coming for the holidays."

"You weren't expecting her?"

"I usually visit her. That way I can see my friends in the Bay Area and leave before my mom starts driving me insane."

"But this year you're staying home?"

"Yeah."

Because of you, Soleil thought to herself.

Whoa.

Where had that come from?

But it was true.

She hadn't planned on it. She hadn't given much thought to the reasons she didn't feel like going to her mom's house. She'd known West was part of it, but she hadn't realized he was the main reason she wasn't leaving town. There was the issue of the baby, too, of her mom not knowing yet, but mostly, staying home was about West.

And of course her mother had gotten her e-mail and taken it as a hint to come to Soleil instead.

West started the car. "I'm looking forward to meeting her," he said, smiling in a way that didn't sit right with Soleil.

"You won't feel that way after she spends an evening with you, railing against the military-industrial complex or explaining how all her poems are really about the inferiority of men."

He smiled that lazy smile of his that never failed to spark desire in her. "I bet she's not as bad as you make her out to be."

"She's worse."

Soleil finally remembered that she'd left the package of crackers in the storage compartment in the door, and she found it and quickly popped another cracker into her mouth.

"Maybe we ought to have some lunch," West said.

"There's a great Thai place a few blocks that way," Soleil said, pointing south.

"Let's do it."

"I'm not sure what your schedule is like for the rest of the day, but if you have time, I'd like to stop at a store, too."

"No problem."

This was all sounding way too domestic and feeling way too claustrophobic for Soleil's taste, especially when she considered the reality of going crib shopping with West. Yet, when contrasted with the thought of her mother's probable reaction to him, she had a rebellious urge to go wild with the whole domestic thing.

She gave him directions to the restaurant, and a few minutes later they were being seated at a table for two next to a window that overlooked the strip-mall parking lot.

"Not so great on ambience," she said, "but the curries are to die for."

"Great." He paused, seeming distracted. "Listen, about your mom, I really would like to meet her. Maybe we could have dinner with my mother and yours both. Sort of, you know, get the two families together."

She tried to imagine lovely, sensible, capable Julia Morgan enduring an entire evening with her arrogant, self-important, whiskey-loving mother.

"I like your mom. I don't think she deserves that kind of suffering."

The waitress arrived then.

"Order for both of us—whatever you think it is good," West said, so she asked for two Thai iced teas, spring rolls and green curry with rice.

After the waitress left the table, Soleil stared at him, trying to decide how to proceed from green curry to what to do with the rest of their lives.

"What?" he asked.

"Oh, nothing."

"My mom really likes you, too, you know," he said.

She nodded, grateful for the change of subject. "That's a compliment. She's one of those pillars of the community that, if anything really bad ever happens, you know she'll be right there, putting civilization back together from scratch."

He laughed without smiling. "She is definitely that, to her own detriment, I think."

"What do you mean?"

"My dad—his health is declining, and he's harassed all his caretakers into quitting, so what does my mom do when she hears about it?"

The waitress showed up with their drinks, and Soleil gave West a questioning look as she began mixing the tea, condensed milk and cream together in her glass.

"She shows up and insists on being his caregiver. Even though they're divorced, and even though he's bound to make her miserable."

"Wow. That's—"

"Nutty," he filled in.

"No, it's sweet. Kind of twisted, but sweet."

West shook his head. "They've been divorced for most of my adult life. It's freaky to see her in his house, serving him omelets and putting up with his crap."

"She's a grown woman. She has her reasons. It's too bad there aren't more people as selfless as her in the world. So what's going on with your dad? You didn't mention anything was wrong with him."

"He's the reason I came home early. He's got Alzheimer's and it's been getting worse in the past few months."

"Oh, God, I'm sorry."

So not only had she dropped a bombshell on him with the surprise pregnancy, but she'd managed to do it when he was going through a major family trauma. What timing. The ball of guilt in her belly grew another few inches.

West took a drink of his own tea, shrugging. After, he said, "It's grim to see him like that."

"The General," Soleil murmured.

She didn't really know West's father, had only met him once, but had heard of him from the time he'd served on the town council a few years ago and frequently caused uproars with his bullheadedness.

"I would have told my mom no way should she be taking care of him, but she's determined to be there until I can find a better situation."

"What does that mean—a better situation?"

He shrugged. "I wish I knew."

"Do you think he needs to go to a nursing home?"

West's gaze turned hard, but his voice came out soft. "He's near that point, sure, but…"

"You can't do it?"

"I also can't leave my mom here to try to manage on her own with Dad. So I'm hoping to find a good caregiver to hire who can't be bullied by my dad."

"Maybe a former drill sergeant?"

He laughed and shook his head, but it was a facade. The slump in his shoulders said everything. She'd never seen West look so defeated as he did right now, and she ached for him.

"There's nothing scarier than seeing someone you thought was invincible for most of your life suddenly falling apart."

"What was your dad like when you were growing up? I mean, I hope he wasn't as much of a dictator as he tried to be on the Promise town council."

Their spring rolls arrived, and Soleil didn't bother acting politely. As soon as she saw the food, she was ravenous. She grabbed a roll, dipped it in sauce and took an enormous bite.

West seemed on the verge of making a joke about her hunger, but must have thought better of it. "I'd say he's mellowed out in recent years, so the guy you saw on the town council was probably a kinder, gentler John Morgan."

"Yikes."

"He used to make us do push-ups if we forgot to say *sir* when addressing him."

"And you willingly joined the military after that?"

He shrugged, half grinning. "I guess it felt familiar."

"And you probably wanted to finally please your dad."

"Something like that. It's always driven me crazy that I care so much what he thinks. I spent so much time pissing him off when I was a kid. Then when I finally had a chance to get out from under his thumb for good, I went right into the air force academy."

Soleil caught the discomfort in his expression, as if he was seeing how transparent his choices were for the first time, and she decided not to push him toward any more self-revelation.

But he continued on his own. "I guess I've never thought about it before, but I must have been desperate to prove something."

"Prove what?"

He frowned. "I've always been proud that I made the Special Forces team after the General told me there was no way I could do it."

"Of course. Why wouldn't you be?"

"Seeing the way my father is now—not himself

anymore… I wish I could let go of those petty feelings."

Thinking of her own mother, Soleil said, "Family relationships rarely bring out the best in us."

Understatement of the year.

He lapsed into silence as he ate a spring roll, and Soleil wondered if she'd ever have the courage to broach the subject that was hanging in the air between them like a deadweight—the baby, their future, what they were going to do…

"So," she said, her throat suddenly tight, "you're happy with your career?"

His gaze searched hers. He wanted to know why she was asking, and she wasn't sure she even knew. "Sure," he said. "I mean, it's my life."

"That's how I feel about the farm," she said, a weird mix of regret and satisfaction plaguing her.

They had such opposite paths in life: he traveled around the world performing covert military operations, while she was rooted firmly to one sacred spot, doing work that affirmed life and encouraged growth. She didn't see how they could ever make raising a child together work.

"We've got the baby to consider," he said.

Whoa, he'd come right out and said it.

"Right," she croaked.

"I have to admit, I never thought about how a family would fit into my career life. After seeing my parents' marriage fall apart, I wasn't in any hurry to get married, or have kids, for that matter."

"Yeah," she said, a film of sweat breaking out on her upper lip. "Me, neither."

"There's no way I can have my own flesh and blood walking around in the world, and not take part in raising her."

"West—" The cold sweat spread to the back of her neck, her chest, her underarms…

"Just listen. You've had five and a half months to figure out how a baby will fit into your life, and I've had a couple of days. But the way I felt in that doctor's office, and the look I saw on your face, you've got to admit we have some common ground here. We both want the best for our baby."

Tears, treacherous tears, sprang to her eyes. Soleil was not the kind of woman who burst into tears over lunch. It had to be the pregnancy hormones. They were making her nuttier and nuttier. She blinked away the dampness and looked out the window.

"Of course," she said.

"I don't know how our parenting her together will look yet, but we owe it to the baby to make whatever compromises it takes to give her a good life with both of her parents."

Soleil forced herself to nod. She couldn't argue with him, but she also couldn't imagine what compromises would get them to a place of harmony. And yet, she wanted to recapture that moment of sheer joy they'd shared while viewing the ultrasound. She wanted to feel that hopeful and happy all the time, not only for a few minutes.

"Maybe you could have someone else run the farm while you move to Colorado—"

A humorless laugh burst from Soleil's throat. She contemplated hurling the last spring roll at his forehead, but no. Happy and hopeful—that's how she was wanted to feel right now.

"Why do you assume I'll be the one making the compromises?" she said as evenly as she could.

He leaned back in his chair, crossing his thickly muscled arms over his chest. Something sparked in his blue eyes. "I'd say we're both compromising there. I'm the one who'd have to put up with you."

He was toying with her temper because starting an argument was easier than working through their differences.

With a Herculean effort, she ignored the bait. "Let's don't go there."

He cocked an eyebrow. "Go where?"

"I don't want to argue with you right now. Let's just, for today, try to get along. Cool?"

"Cool," he said quietly.

His gaze lingered too long on her. He had a way of looking at her, the way he did now, that turned her into a fool, made her a quivering mass of hormones that wanted nothing more than to be in his presence.

And she hated—absolutely hated—that he wielded such power over her.

She turned her attention to her tea, stirring it even though the drink no longer needed it.

"So," he said, "I get to meet your mother soon."

She forced a smile. Meeting the parents was a particularly horrifying idea when it would involve admitting at the same time that they were accidentally knocked up.

She, the social worker, the one who lectured teen girls about taking charge of their reproduction, using birth control and making smart choices, should have known better.

"Um, yeah."

"Do you worry about turning out too much like your mother?"

"Sure. Especially now that I'll be a single mother, too."

West's expression hardened, and she realized too late that she'd ventured into controversial territory again. *He* didn't intend for her to be a single mother.

"How about you?" she asked, to smooth over the awkwardness. "Afraid of turning into your father?"

"Absolutely."

"It's a valid fear," she said.

"Gee, thanks."

"No problem." She grinned. "I mean, I'm sure you're not any more like him than I am like my mother…except that in some ways, I'm very much like her, and it scares the hell out of me."

"Why?"

"Because she's crazy."

"Crazy how?"

"You'll see when she gets here."

He didn't look satisfied with that answer.

"Let's just say it sounds like you experienced the opposite of my upbringing. And unlike your dad, my mom hasn't mellowed out at all in her old age."

West made a face, and Soleil turned her attention to the curry that was arriving at the table.

It was true, she recognized too much of her mother in herself. When she had to spend actual time with Anne their likenesses, as well as their differences, became all too painfully clear.

The very thought of her mother's arrival nearly made her lose her appetite. Nearly, but not quite.

CHAPTER NINE

As they walked from the Thai restaurant to the baby store, West checked the messages on his cell phone, relieved to see there weren't any urgent calls from his mother about the General. There was a call from his assignment officer, but he didn't want to know yet what that one was about. He slipped the phone into his pocket, struck by how quickly his life had transformed into one he barely recognized.

A week ago, he'd been in Colorado, puzzling over how he'd get his father's caregiver situation squared away so that he could go off to Afghanistan or wherever his next assignment sent him. He'd been thinking he'd pressure his two brothers over the holidays to step in and take some responsibility for the situation—not his mother—and he'd had no idea how profoundly his life was about to change.

He'd even been stupid enough to wonder if he might hook up with Soleil again, spend some more time with her. If he'd only known.

He surveyed the store, aisle after aisle of cutesy baby paraphernalia, and he again had the urge to go hunt a wild boar. Soleil, for her part, looked just as bewildered. She stepped tentatively forward, then stopped, frowning at a display of how-to books, each cover cutesier than the last.

"God," she muttered, picking up a book with a picture of a pregnant woman in a rocking chair on the cover. "How lame do they think women are?"

West picked up a hefty tome entitled *The Breast-feeding Book*, half wondering what it had to say in all those pages that he hadn't already learned in that three-page article. Soleil eyed his selection but said nothing.

"So we're here for a crib, right?" he asked as he returned the book to the shelf.

"Right," she said, fumbling in her purse and pulling out a list. "And a few other things."

"What are these things?" West picked up a U-shaped pillow decorated with pictures of daisies and put it up to his face. "For sleeping facedown?"

Soleil laughed. "It's a nursing pillow. Didn't you learn all about them in that breast-feeding article?"

"Wait a sec. How does this thing work?" He held it down at his waist, then squeezed it on like a life preserver.

"You wear it like that while you're sitting down, and it supports the baby and your arms. It's a comfort thing, I guess."

"For someone who reads the *New Yorker,* you sure know a lot about weird-looking baby equipment."

She rolled her eyes at him and turned her attention back to the cribs. "We didn't come here to buy that," she said.

"So…are you planning to breast-feed?"

"Sure, why not. I'll finally get to put these inconvenient things to use," she said, motioning at her chest.

"Trust me, those are anything but inconvenient."

"You've never gone jogging with them."

"I would if I could," he joked, and she finally cracked a smile.

Watching her in profile as she studied the selection of cribs, he felt overcome with a feeling he'd never had for her before. He'd always found her attractive and exciting, but now, the way they'd settled into this sort of companionable day, even with the momentous stuff that had happened, she felt like… like a friend.

She felt like not only someone he wanted to sleep with, but someone he wanted to hang out with, talk to and solicit opinions from.

He appreciated that she was making an effort to get along. And he, for his part, was trying his best not to goad her into any arguments for the fireworks value. Besides, he was in no mood for games lately.

"What do you think of this one?" she said, indicating a mahogany bed with simple lines and a sweeping sort of sleighlike headboard and footboard.

"It's beautiful," he said. "Is that the one you want?"

She smiled and nodded. "Yeah, I think so."

"Let's get it."

They went in search of a salesperson to help them, and along the way, West eyed the mind-boggling amount of baby stuff to be bought.

"Should we, uh, be buying all this other stuff, too? Because I can cover the tab. It's the least I can do—"

"Not yet," she said. "There'll probably be a shower in another month or two, and people will give us gifts. Once we see what everyone's given us, then we can go shopping for the stuff we still need."

There was that word. *We.* She'd used it three times. And *us.*

He liked hearing her talk that way, but he also knew she only meant it in the simplest sense. She wasn't suggesting anything by it.

Or was she?

The way today had gone, how could she not start thinking of them as a couple? They'd seen their baby for the first time together. They were shopping for cribs now.

This was heavy-duty stuff.

His throat went tight, and he tried to stuff down his feelings as Soleil talked to a salesperson about having the crib delivered to her house.

He could feel his future taking shape for the first time. Until now, he'd lived his life in the moment. He'd lived for the thrill of his work and nothing more, but now…

Now he had something bigger to live for. And his baby was depending on him to make a plan, to think about the future, to be responsible in a way he'd never been called upon to be before.

He knew what he had to do. So many things made sense now that didn't before. Soleil and him—they had a lot to decide, and at the same time, all the decisions were obvious.

He didn't want to play it cool. He wanted to make sure Soleil understood that they were supposed to be together. No more taking his time, giving her space, or any of that crap.

He was going to make them a family, the way they were supposed to be.

SOLEIL ALLOWED the motion of the car to lull her into a trance as they rode back to Promise. She was surprised at what a good day she and West had had together. She could even imagine them working well together as parents. No, that was probably pregnancy hormones getting the best of her.

She cast a glance at him, then looked away again quickly before he could make eye contact.

Could they be happy together?

Was it really so preposterous an idea?

Soleil believed romantic notions were mostly societal constructs designed to keep men and women in traditional roles. They persisted because they served to keep civilization intact. They didn't necessarily serve any individual—and certainly not any female individual—well.

But what about the baby?

Her gut wrenched. *That* was the reason the societal constructs existed. Family units were good for raising babies. The individual was supposed to be overshadowed by the needs of the child.

She felt again as if some vital part of herself was slipping away. What if she ceased to recognize herself at all?

If she was committed to West, would any part of the real her be able to survive?

He was the strongest man she'd ever been with. And, she had to admit, she was used to being the strong, dominant one in the relationship. That was part of the reason she and West had butted heads so frequently in the summer.

But was her sense of self really so fragile that she couldn't be involved with a strong man who didn't agree with her on every damn issue?

Hell, no.

"You're being awfully quiet over there. Anything bothering you?" West asked, breaking the silence.

"Oh, um, no."

He glanced in her direction but said nothing.

"Okay, yeah. I'm thinking about, you know, how things are going to work, once the baby arrives."

"Yeah?"

"It's complicated," she said, stating the obvious.

"It doesn't have to be."

Maybe he was right.

"I don't know," she said quietly.

"It's been nice, spending the day with you. Thank you for inviting me."

"Of course, you can come to the next—" She stopped, realizing too late that he wouldn't be around for the next one.

"You can call and tell me about it if I'm not here."

If I'm not here.

"What do you mean?"

He shrugged. "I don't know. I mean, we have to work out some way to share custody of the baby, right?"

"But you're in the air force."

"I don't know. Maybe I could get assigned to Travis Air Force Base. Then I'd only be a few hours away and could commute here on weekends."

"Really? That's a possibility?"

"I have no idea. Honestly, it would probably be a career-ending move for me. I need to go overseas next to stay competitive for promotion."

Soleil kept her gaze glued on the passing scenery. Her eyes stung, though. She didn't like to hear West putting his career first, which was ridiculous since she wasn't sure she wanted to hear him say he was moving to Promise, either.

"What about you?" he said. "What does your ideal future look like?"

She sighed. "It used to look pretty much like my present looks now. I love the farm. It's been the happiest place in my life ever since I was a little kid visiting my grandparents there."

"So you want your own child to experience it, too."

"Of course."

"I don't know what my ideal future looks like now. With a kid, do you even get to hope for ideal? Or do you simply hope for healthy and safe?"

"I've never had to think about it before."

"Neither have I."

In that, at least, they were united.

But it was cold comfort, and Soleil didn't dare to hope for anything more right now.

CHAPTER TEN

WHEN JULIA'S DOORBELL rang at exactly six the night of her first date with Frank her heart leaped from her chest into her throat. She paused in the foyer and took a few deep, cleansing breaths, but they did little to calm her nerves. Then she opened the door, saw Frank standing there, clutching a bouquet of lavender, and the tension drained away.

"Hello," she said.

"These are for you." He smiled, handing her the flowers, and she realized he was as nervous as she had been.

This realization had the effect of calming her even more. She was charmed by the fact that he cared enough to be nervous. Inhaling the scent of the lavender, Julia stepped aside and invited Frank in.

Then she wondered for a moment if she was making some horrible mistake. Wasn't this how women ended up in the news, unsuspecting victims of violent crimes perpetrated by men they'd met on the Internet? If she closed the door, she'd officially be home alone with this stranger, and—

No, she had to stop this. She was being paranoid.

He looked around. "This is nice. Have you been here long?"

"Ten years," she said. "I bought my condo after the divorce."

He gazed up at the high, slanted ceiling with its wood beams. Then his gaze went to the wall, where Julia's one great extravagance hung. It was an etching she'd bought a few years ago when she'd stopped teaching, a retirement gift to herself.

"Wow, a Lily Keith?" He crossed the room to get a closer look at the stark black-and-white image of a city bursting with life.

"Yes. She's one of my favorite artists."

"You have great taste. Did you know she has an exhibit in San Francisco right now at the MOMA?"

Julia blinked. She had to keep reminding herself that Frank was an artist and was therefore interested in art—not only football or hunting or the rest of the stereotypical male interests about which she had little to say.

"Oh? I had no idea."

He grinned. "Would you like to see it?"

"I'd love to."

"Tonight?"

Julia laughed in surprise. "I doubt we could make it to the city before the museum closes."

He smiled. "Good point. But soon, we should go."

She liked his spontaneity. She needed more of that in her life.

He looked back at the etching, and Julia took the opportunity to study him. He was dressed a little more formally this evening than he had been the first time she'd seen him, in a brown leather coat, a white button-down shirt and a pair of brown khakis that managed to somehow look relaxed and creative rather than stuffy and conformist. She loved that he had a touch of style, on top of being an attractive man.

She was already feeling silly for worrying that he might be someone to fear. He seemed as if he belonged in her home, as if he were an old friend who'd always been part of the landscape.

"You have a flair for decorating," he said as he surveyed the room.

"Oh, I just have too much time on my hands," she said, waving away his compliment, though secretly, she was pleased.

He eyed her. "I doubt that."

"I was thinking we could walk to the town center and have a drink, then wander around to find a place that looks good for dinner."

"Sounds perfect," Frank said, smiling. "I don't come out here to Promise enough. I've always loved this town."

Julia got her coat from the closet and put it on. "The first time I came here, I knew it was where I wanted to live," she said as they walked outside and she locked the door.

"Where did you grow up?"

"Oh, all over. My father was in the military, as was my ex-husband. I lived everywhere from Korea to Tulsa in my first eighteen years."

They began walking toward town. Outside, it was dark, but the streetlights in the condo complex illuminated the way out to the main road. The bittersweet scent of the redwoods that grew across from Julia's unit permeated the air. She loved being able to walk everywhere she needed to go, while still living right next to the lake, too.

"That must have been difficult, moving all the time."

"I didn't like it much as a kid, making friends then having to leave them behind and make new ones, but I coped. When I left home and went to college, I got pretty antsy living in the same location for four whole years."

"And when you were married?"

"Oh, by that time I'd accepted that I didn't know how to stay in one place. Marrying a military man seemed like the perfect situation."

Frank shook his head. "But you've been here in Promise for quite a while, right? How do you manage now?"

"I went to therapy for a while before and after my divorce, and I realized leaving was a coping mechanism. It was a distraction from things about my life I wasn't happy with."

"So once you dealt with those things, you didn't need to keep moving on?"

"Yes. I could sit still."

"Must have been a relief to figure that out."

"It was," she said quietly. It didn't seem right to discuss anything surrounding her divorce so early in this relationship, but she supposed vague references were occasionally okay.

"How about your divorce? Was it a very messy one?"

Unless, of course, he asked.

"Aren't they all?" she said.

"I hear of occasional smooth ones."

It occurred to Julia that she'd been letting Frank ask most of the questions. "And yours? Smooth or rough?"

"Believe it or not, we split pretty congenially. It had been a long time coming, and we both knew it, I think."

"Yes, it's easier if no one is caught by surprise."

"I'm afraid the kids were surprised by it. That's my only regret."

"How old were they?"

"Twenty and twenty-two, but they were still pretty unhappy."

Julia sighed, thinking of her own kids. "My sons didn't seem to care that much one way or the other. Probably because they're boys—they tend to keep their feelings to themselves."

"Were they grown when you split up?"

"Yes, all three were out of the house. Once we didn't have raising the boys to distract us from each other anymore, and we were settled in one place finally, there wasn't any getting around the fact that we made each other miserable."

Or, to put it more accurately, there was no denying that she no longer wanted to be married to her ex-husband. He'd seemed happy enough with the status quo. But that was a detail for another time.

"That's exactly what happened to us. Well, and my ex-wife, Linda, had always wanted to live in the city and have a cosmopolitan life. The girls had been my excuse for staying put, and when I didn't have that excuse anymore, she picked up and left. We'd grown apart in our interests and priorities, that's all."

She didn't hear any bitterness in his voice, and she was glad of that. It also spoke well of him that he took some ownership for the marriage problems.

"And did Linda remarry?"

"Yes, she's with a nice man and seems happy. I'm glad to see her moving on."

"I thought we might have a drink here," Julia said as they reached the main intersection in town. They stood in front of a lovely little wine bar, warmly lit and inviting.

"Looks perfect." Without a moment's resistance, Frank opened the door and waited for her to go inside.

She loved that he could let her select a place without having a debate over it. And she loved that he listened. And asked questions. And seemed interested in the answers.

If she wasn't careful, she feared she'd start falling for him all too fast. Already she felt a delicious tingle of excitement down low in her belly, a sensation she hadn't experienced in so many years, she'd forgotten it existed until now.

No, there had to be something wrong with Frank, some fatal flaw lurking about waiting to pop up and surprise her when she least expected it. She had to keep her eyes open wide.

The place was sparsely populated with customers. They found chairs at the end of the bar, away from the chatter of the nearest couple, and a bartender brought them menus.

"Are you a white- or a red-wine lady?"

"I like both, but I think I'm in the mood for red tonight."

"Maybe we could each get a glass and try two different reds?"

"Sure." She read over the menu, and once they'd made their selections and ordered, Julia took a moment to look around.

The other couples were mostly younger and hipper looking than her and Frank, but she felt at ease.

"So," she said, "how have you managed to stay single all this time?"

Not that she expected him to tell the truth, but she figured she might get some hint of it with a well-timed question.

Frank flashed a wry grin. "I've dated a bit, but there has only been one serious relationship since my divorce. We were together for a year before figuring out we weren't right for each other." He paused and shrugged. "Since then I haven't met anyone I wanted to share my life with."

Julia nodded. Boy, did she ever relate. "It's hard after having a long marriage, isn't it?"

"When you've already spent a lifetime making things work."

"I was surprised how much I've come to value my independence." Julia's face warmed. Was she supposed to say such things on a first date? Was it considered gauche to point out the downsides of relationships to a potential boyfriend?

Oh, who the hell cared? She didn't want to play games. She wanted to be honest, damn the consequences.

To her pleasant surprise, Frank simply nodded in agreement. "Yes, exactly."

The bartender brought the wine they'd ordered and gave each of them a taste before pouring the glasses. The spicy smooth taste of the merlot went straight to Julia's head, and she found herself warming even more to Frank even before the wine had any real chance to affect her.

"I hope I'm not sounding old and bitter," Julia said in a conspiratorial tone, leaning in close.

"Not at all. Do you feel old and bitter?"

"No. And you?"

"I did until I walked into that coffee shop and saw you sitting there."

"Oh?"

Frank sipped his wine, his eyes twinkling. "Have you ever gotten into a funk and not even recognized the landscape until something good happened to shake you out of it?"

She gave the matter some thought and recalled the moment she'd seen Frank's online profile. It had created an instant sense of dissatisfaction—as if her life suddenly was less for not knowing him. "I have, now that you mention it."

"Meeting you shook me out of my funk, so thank you."

Julia thought of chiming in with a "Me, too," but it would have been the equivalent of heaping sugar on top of a hot-fudge sundae. Instead, she kept her mouth shut and basked in feeling the best she'd felt in years—decades, perhaps.

CHAPTER ELEVEN

SOLEIL OPENED one eye and squinted at the clock.

The sound of a horn honking at nine-fifteen in the morning was not a welcome one. This was supposed to be a day of sleeping in, being lazy, relishing her aloneness and nothing-to-do-ness for the first time in several months.

She wasn't expecting any deliveries, or visitors, or—

Her mother.

She sat up in bed to peer out the window, and sure enough, the telltale sight of a white Honda in the driveway greeted her.

Oh God, oh God, oh God.

Wasn't her mother supposed to arrive tomorrow? Definitely tomorrow. She was sure if it, because she'd been certain to mark her calendar with the date her mother had said she was arriving.

But here Anne was, getting out of the car, slamming the door, walking back to the trunk and opening it...

Soleil flopped down on her pillow and groaned. Maybe she could not answer the door.

Except her car was parked out front, and she'd only be delaying the inevitable.

So she got out of bed, went to the bathroom, washed her hands and splashed a little water on her face. Then she grabbed her bathrobe and shrugged it on before heading downstairs to open the door.

"Hello?" she could hear her calling from outside.

"Just a sec," she called as she unlocked and opened the door that her mother was urgently knocking on. "I thought you were getting here tomorrow."

She was face-to-face with her mother. Soleil had to admit Anne looked good with her long white hair and faintly olive skin that accented her pale green eyes. Soleil had definitely inherited her height and eye color from her mother, which caused her to briefly consider what traits her own daughter would share.

"My schedule changed, so I decided to surprise you!" Anne smiled and was extending her arms for a hug when her gaze dropped to Soleil's belly, and her expression transformed to one of utter shock and disbelief.

"You're—" She stopped, as if she couldn't say the truth out loud.

"Pregnant," Soleil filled in for her.

"But… When did… And who…?"

She stared at Soleil's belly as if the answers might be down there.

"Five months and three weeks or so. I'm due in early May."

"Oh, my. I'm… Why didn't you tell me?" She finally pieced together an entire sentence.

"I was going to. It's been kind of nutty, and I thought… I guess I planned to surprise you for Christmas." Sort of true. She had entertained the idea of showing up for the holidays and surprising her mother with the news.

"Well, you've certainly surprised me. Help me with these bags, then you can fill me in over coffee."

Soleil picked up the closer of the two bags, already dreading how long her mother must have been planning to stay if two medium-size suitcases were required.

She carried the bag down the hallway to the nicest of the guest rooms and placed it inside the door. This had been her grandparents' bedroom once upon a time—the master suite of the house. But Soleil preferred the upstairs bedroom with the soaring view for herself, which had been her mother's room as a little girl.

"Can you believe I was conceived *and* born in this room?" her mother said, shaking her head and giving a bit too much information as usual. "Probably on that exact bed."

It was true the same bedroom furniture that Gram and Grampa Bishop had left behind was still here. Soleil hadn't seen any point in moving it, when it suited the room.

This reminded Soleil of something she'd been forgetting to mention for months. "I went through the attic not too long ago and found some of Gram's things. I'll have to show them to you later and see if you want any of it."

"I've got enough of my own crap," Anne answered as she dropped a suitcase on the bed and unzipped the outer pocket. From it she withdrew a silver flask, which surely contained whiskey.

"It's not even ten in the morning. Isn't it a little early to be drinking?"

"It's cold as hell out there and I just found out that my only daughter is knocked up. I'll be having my coffee Irish."

Soleil sighed but knew better than to argue. Anne had always been a heavy drinker and probably always would be.

Soleil went to the kitchen and made a pot of decaf, which her mother would complain about. Too bad. She'd have to get over it.

Anne followed her. "So, who's the baby's father?"

"Not anyone you'd know."

"Of course I wouldn't, since you seem to have completely shut me out of your life."

"Right, Mom. You can spare me the vitriol."

She got the cream out of the fridge and put it on the table with a bottle of honey.

"I've cut all sugar and dairy out of my diet," her mother said.

"It's not sugar, it's honey."

"I'm seeing an acupuncturist who has me on a cleansing diet. I'm only allowed to eat vegetables and lean protein for the next month."

"And whiskey?"

"I make allowances for a few necessities," Anne said with a flourish of her hand.

Soleil tried not to roll her eyes.

"So tell me all about him."

"The baby? I haven't met her yet."

"*Her?* You know you're having a girl? That's wonderful! But you're avoiding my question."

"The baby's father is West Morgan. We're not in a relationship, but he does want to be involved in the baby's life."

Her mother watched her for a few moments, silent, a half smile playing on her lips. "I guess all my feminist ranting really did get through to you, didn't it?"

"What do you mean?"

"Here you are, a self-sufficient woman, getting ready to start a family all on your own. You'll be co-parents or whatever they're calling it these days. I'm so proud of you, dear."

This was the reaction Soleil expected from her mother, so she had no idea why she suddenly felt as if her head was going to explode.

"I just wish you'd told me you were planning to have a baby. I'd have loved to share all this with you from the start."

"Mom, I didn't exactly plan this."

"Honestly, I never saw you as a potential breeder. You pour so much of your energy into saving the world—"

"A potential breeder?"

"Well, now you're an actual breeder."

"Thanks. That's lovely."

The coffee stopped perking, a welcome distraction. Soleil got out two cups and poured one for each of them, then carried the cups to the table and sat.

"Don't you use birth control?"

"Of course I do. It's capable of malfunctioning, you know."

Anne uncapped her flask and poured a healthy splash into the coffee. Then another.

Soleil winced. "How can you drink that without even a little cream or something?"

Her mother shrugged. "One sip at a time. It goes down quite easily."

Sure, if you're used to drinking your whiskey straight from the flask.

"Anyway, you'll meet West. He's supposed to come here tomorrow to help me put the baby's crib together."

"You know, I'll never understand you. You'd think you'd want to share this time of your life with me."

"Of course I want to share it with you," Soleil said, trying not to grit her teeth.

"But? You're being intentionally spiteful to punish me for imagined grievances from childhood?"

Soleil halted in the middle of adding cream to her

coffee. "I don't think this is a good way to be starting our visit," she said as calmly as she could, though it came out sounding as tense as she felt.

Her mother leaned back in her seat, crossed her slender arms over her chest and fixed a narrow-eyed gaze on Soleil. She was ready to battle.

"I'm *not* going to sit around and pretend everything is okay when my own daughter is concealing the most important facts of her life from me," Anne said in the not-quite-steady voice of the clinically unbalanced. "Have you ever known me to play nice about such things? How did you think I'd react?"

"I thought you'd react like a crazy person no matter when I told you, which is why I put it off!"

She slammed the carton of cream down on the table and a splash of it sloshed out of the spout. Then she pushed back her chair and prepared to storm out of the room.

But that was her adolescent self reacting. Grownup Soleil hated to run away and prolong an argument. She preferred to stand her ground and work things out. But that never quite seemed to create peace with her mother. Instead, it was more like an exercise in pounding her head against the wall.

Anne sat silently perusing her response options, one eyebrow cocked as if daring Soleil to leave.

"You have no idea how hurt I am," Anne finally said, her tone taking on a note of self-pity. "I thought we were better friends than this."

The guilt trip. One of Soleil's least favorite of her mother's weapons. "We're not friends. We're a parent and child, but I have no idea which of us is supposed to be the child right now."

Her mother eschewed the spiked coffee and took a long drink from her flask. "I'm going to my room to rest, and when I come back, I'll expect an apology," she said, standing. "And I want to meet this West person sooner rather than later, since he's going to be part of our happy little family now."

He's not going to be part of the family, Soleil wanted to argue, but that wasn't exactly correct. Her mother was, at least about this, right. As she watched Anne leave the room, doing what Soleil had deemed too immature, she knew she was in for a worse than usual visit if she didn't find a way to get her mother focused on something else.

It was as if without even knowing it, Anne was conspiring with West to turn Soleil's life into something she didn't want it to be.

Conspiring with West...

This gave Soleil an idea. Maybe he'd be the distraction to get both of them off her back.

She drank her coffee, cleaned up the kitchen and once she'd given her mother time to fall asleep for a nap, she crept upstairs to the nursery, where she sat in the middle of the floor to contemplate the view. This room was her favorite in the house now, thanks to the purple wall color she'd chosen. She came here to sit and not exactly meditate, but let her mind trip over all the facts of her life, and speculate about the future.

For a least an hour now, her mother had been holed up in the guest room, napping or, whatever it was she was doing. Composing an angry poem about what a bad daughter Soleil was? It wouldn't have been the first time.

One of her mother's more famous poems—one that had shown up in quite a few feminist anthologies over the years—was entitled "Stranger of Mine."

Stranger not as in strange, but as in, someone you don't know. As in Soleil, apparently.

She'd never asked her mother about the poem. It had been composed when Soleil was in her teen years, but she hadn't seen it until thumbing through her freshman anthology in college.

The poem's theme of alienation between mother and child had felt like an insult all those years ago. As if her mother had announced to the world that she didn't really know her daughter, without ever telling Soleil herself.

What was not to know?

Was her mother merely being dramatic?

That was a distinct possibility, but the very fact that the notion had occurred to Anne only served to drive Soleil further away.

She wanted to have an entirely different relationship with her own daughter. She wanted to be a lov-

ing, fun, strict but kind mother. A sane mother. Someone her daughter could trust to keep it real.

She would be all those things. She was certain she
could trust herself to do at least that for her child.

But what else could she do? Could she swallow
who she was and give her baby a live-in father? Or
give up the farm and go play air force wife in God-
knows-where?

No way.

She was just as certain that she couldn't do that.

CHAPTER TWELVE

A DAY AFTER her mother's arrival, Soleil was tense and counting the days until Anne would leave. Which would have been a lot easier if she wasn't in Promise for an open-ended visit.

She'd disappeared in the morning, on her way to a day at the local hot springs, where she'd scheduled a massage and was attending some kind of relaxation workshop.

If it meant she'd learn how to relax without the aid of alcohol, Soleil was all for it. And she was relieved to have her mother gone for West's visit to assemble the crib.

"So, this is the baby's room," Soleil said as she led West into the bedroom next to her own.

It was the smallest bedroom in the house and would work perfectly as a nursery. She'd originally intended to put off creating a nursery until later, once she'd figured out other more important details of her impending motherhood—like how to tell the baby's father she was pregnant, and how to take care of a baby and run the farm at the same time. Then she'd dreamed of painting the baby's room purple, so she'd done it.

Now, with West commandeering her life, she could ponder things like where to place the crib in the room, and what view the baby might enjoy best.

Her baby girl.

Preparing the nursery was one more step along the path to the baby becoming a real live person, complete with name and favorite foods and a set of eyes through which to view the world as no one else did.

"Great location. We— I mean, *you* will be able to hear her when she wakes up."

Soleil bit her tongue, choosing to ignore his little slip. Maybe it had been an honest mistake, and not yet another example of him insinuating himself into her world. Either way, because he'd been so nice about wanting to help out around the farm when she needed it, and because she was enjoying his company more than she'd thought she would, she was playing the diplomat.

When she didn't say anything, he apparently took her silence as a sign that she was upset. "I didn't mean to suggest—"

"It's okay. I know you're trying to work your way into my bed," she joked, but as soon as the words were out of her mouth, they had an unintended effect.

They shined light on a fact she'd been working hard to ignore—that she was still attracted to him physically.

Wildly attracted, in spite of their differences, in spite of her ever-increasing girth, in spite of the stress of the holidays. It had always been her problem.

West smiled, a little too knowingly for her comfort. And, in that infuriating way he often had, he let the awkwardness hang there in the air between them, not saying a word.

"Okay," Soleil said. "There's the bed. I'm going to start the second coat of paint. Just let me know if you need any help putting that puppy together."

He eyed the huge cardboard box. "Do you have any tools inside, or are they all in the barn?"

"In the kitchen there's a tool set in the first drawer to the left of the sink."

He disappeared down the hallway, and Soleil put the old T-shirt on that she'd been using for painting. She turned on the radio, tuned in to the local station that was currently playing a tribute to Joni Mitchell, to save them from any more awkward silences. She pried the lid off the paint can, poured more paint into the pan, then started applying the second coat.

They worked without talking for a while, and Soleil tried to get lost in the rhythm of painting. It was something she normally enjoyed doing, finding it meditative and physical in a satisfying way, but today she felt West's presence like a wild animal that she had to constantly be on the lookout for.

"Could you give me a hand with this part?" West

asked, and Soleil turned to see that not only did he have his shirt off—dear Lord—but that he'd managed to put together most of the bed already.

Some part of her was disappointed that he might be leaving soon.

"Sure." She put down the paint roller and wiped her hands on her stained T-shirt.

"I need you to help me get these two pieces into the headboard, and hold it while I screw them in place."

"You're fast," she said, trying to think what else she could ask him to do, and simultaneously berating herself for wanting to keep him around.

"This was easier than it looked," he said as he reached for the screwdriver.

His arm brushed against Soleil's, and a ripple of pleasure traveled from her arm down her chest and past her belly to the apex of her legs.

She shook off the hot flash and forced herself to focus on the bed. The baby bed. The bed for their baby. The one she was very pregnant with.

They guided the final pieces of the crib together while Soleil crouched on the ground. She held the supports still as West screwed them to the headboard, and she tried not to stare at the way his jaw muscle flexed as he clenched his teeth in concentration.

The faint dusting of freckles on his shoulder was what did her in. That shoulder, well muscled, leading down to flexing biceps and triceps, which led to a hard forearm sprinkled with brown hair, which led to large, capable hands that were alternately gentle and teasing or firm and demanding…

Those freckles, she'd seen them up close and kissed them each in turn. She'd dug her teeth into the skin there as he'd made love to her, urgent, almost at climax.

She had nothing but the best of associations with those freckles, those shoulders, those arms, those hands. Not to mention the broad, perfect chest and the flat, rippling belly.

The day she'd found out she was pregnant she'd promised herself that she wouldn't ever lose control sexually again. She'd sworn she would never let lust get the best of her. She'd be responsible, restrained… She'd only make love to a man when they were in a committed relationship, using at least two forms of birth control.

But now she was as knocked up as she was ever going to be, and it wasn't clear whether she'd ever be in a committed relationship again. It wasn't clear if she'd ever have the time or energy before she hit menopause to date or have a relationship, when she was going to be so busy running the farm and taking care of her child.

What if West was her last real chance to get laid?

And what if it wasn't even a chance? What if he didn't want to be with her now that she was shaped like a cartoon character?

"You're looking awfully serious. What're you

thinking about?" West asked as he finished the second bed support and checked to see that it was secure.

He had remarkable timing.

"I was thinking about the characters on children's shows, and how adults hate them."

"I think some of them are kind of cute."

Truly remarkable timing.

"So this is it? The bed's done?"

He nodded.

She started to stand, and the change in her center of gravity set her off balance for a moment. West caught her elbow and steadied her, but instead of taking away his hand once she was fully upright, he lingered, caressing first her arm, then her lower back.

The contact was more than her hormone-addled libido could take. She turned toward him. They were only inches apart. Close enough to kiss.

"Thanks," she said. "For putting the crib together."

"Anytime."

"I'm hoping I won't need another crib anytime soon," she said, but she got the distinct sense that he wasn't really listening now, because he was staring intently at her mouth as if he had a mission.

So now she had to step away, or she was going to kiss him. She needed to take one step backward, then another, and another, until they were a chaste distance apart. She had to remember her vow about no more knocking boots with guys she wasn't in love with.

He leaned down and kissed her, and she turned into

a puddle. His kiss was soft, lips barely brushing hers at first, then lingering, asking if he should continue.

Yes, he should definitely continue.

She reached up and twined her fingers in his hair, pulling him closer as she turned his sweet, gentle kiss into something animal and urgent.

He pulled her closer, in that I'm-in-command way he had, and it all came back to her. The way they moved together, a perfectly choreographed dance, the way their bodies fit together so divinely, the way he knew how to find the places where she ached the most and drive her crazy with teasing and coaxing and pleasuring.

He was the best lover she'd ever had.

And, hallelujah, they were kissing.

Her eyes closed, she felt as if no time had passed between the past summer and now, until she tried to grind her pelvis against him and came up against the barrier of her belly, round and protruding.

It definitely wasn't the summer.

She tugged at his hair a bit, pulling him back just enough so that she could talk. "I can't get pregnant now," she whispered. "I mean, since I already am."

"I haven't had any other lovers since—"

"Neither have I," she said.

He looked relieved.

"Is that what we're doing?" he asked.

"We're not exactly painting the walls. I mean, unless you don't want to—"

"I definitely want to." He ended the discussion by kissing her again as he slid his hands up her shirt, under both her T-shirt and the sweatshirt she wore under it, straight to bare skin.

His cool touch turned her skin to gooseflesh, and when he reached her bra and undid it with one flick of his fingers, she said a little silent prayer of thanks. He slid his hands around to her breasts and cupped them, and she gave a little gasp.

She was humming, a live wire, electric with the desire coursing through her, more aroused than she'd ever been in her life.

It had to be the pregnancy hormones. If he tried to put the brakes on now, or had second thoughts, she feared she might later be compared to a black widow in the newspaper story about how she'd killed her lover.

"Let's go to your bedroom," he said.

She didn't need an invitation. "Yeah," she said, then dragged him in that direction.

CHAPTER THIRTEEN

Soleil had always been a passionate lover, but her enthusiasm now was unprecedented. West almost laughed at the way she'd grabbed him a few minutes ago and dragged him in here.

He'd no more than blinked before she was unfastening his pants and he was kicking them aside. While part of him wanted to put on the brakes and slow them down enough so that he could savor the experience, the part of him that was actually in control wasn't about to slow down anything.

He wanted her as badly as she wanted him, except he was pretty sure he didn't have the same glazed look of determination she had.

Now he was fumbling with her shirts, trying to tug them off of her, except she seemed to be resisting.

"Wait," she said, breaking their kiss. "I, uh, I'm wearing maternity pants…and panties."

"So?"

Her look of distress turned to a wry grin. "I don't want you to see them."

"Why?"

"Because they nearly come up to my armpits."

West recalled the fabric his hand had brushed over on the way to her breasts. At the time he hadn't thought much of it, but now he laughed, imagining her distress.

"I don't care. I'm aroused by you, not what you're wearing."

She cocked one skeptical eyebrow. "Oh, yeah?"

"Let me see."

He tried to lift up her shirts again, and she swatted his hand away. But he grabbed her hand, then caught the other one in his hand and tried to grab her shirts again as she wiggled away.

"Let go. I'm going to the bathroom to get undressed." But she was laughing now, a little too hard to fight him off effectively.

He backed her up to the bed and toppled her onto it, then climbed on her and pinned her hands over her head.

"Let's see what we have here," he said, taking his time about the big reveal.

Tears streamed from the corners of her eyes now, she was laughing so hard. "Stop!" she cried, but he wasn't about to.

He grasped the hems of her shirts and pulled them up. Beneath was a big navy blue stretchy fabric panel that extended from her crotch all the way to the top of her rib cage.

"Wow," he said. "Those are cool."

She tried to pry her arms free, to no avail. "I hate you," she said between giggles.

"And what do we have underneath?" he said as he tugged down the elastic waist of the jeans and found a pair of white panties with a waistline nearly as high as the pants.

"You are so dead."

"Mmm, granny panties. Those are hot."

"Dead! As a doorknob!"

"Why don't they make pants like this for men, too? You can have a big meal and don't even need to do any unbuttoning or unzipping to make room. I'm thinking these will sell big."

"Yeah, the guys who wear them will never get laid again, so food will be their only pleasure anyway."

He caught her eye. They were both smiling, and he could hardly believe he was so close to her now, touching her anywhere he wanted. He'd been trying not to dream of this for months.

He slid his hand up beneath her shirts again, brushing the underside of her breast with his fingertips. He watched as her eyes fluttered shut, and her expression went from amused to nearly rapturous.

Then he leaned in close and kissed her as he tugged down the waist of her pants, eliminating whatever embarrassment she might have felt by simply not looking.

When he let go of her wrists, she tugged her pants the rest of the way down and he stopped kissing her long enough to pull off her shirts and bra before she changed her mind.

Now she was naked before him. Her once-thin body had been transformed into a whole new landscape. Here a mountain range of full, lush breasts, there a valley of smooth skin, and beyond, a round hill where flat plains had once been.

"Beautiful," he said, and it was true.

She was beautiful in a whole new way than she'd been before. She was an image as ancient as humankind, a lovely round fertility goddess in all her brown naked glory.

His erection strained toward her, ready to explore new territory. West didn't want to wait another minute to remind himself what it was like to be inside her, but he also had never made love to a pregnant woman before, and wasn't sure if any precautions were supposed to be taken. Was missionary position safe? Would he squash the baby? Would things be painful? He felt like an idiot even having to wonder.

She sensed his hesitation.

"What?"

"Is it okay to—"

"Of course it is." She sat up, and before he knew it they'd switched positions, her on top, him lying on his back as she straddled his hips.

His erection brushed against her, and she let out a little gasp. She was hot and wet, fully aroused, as he was. He grasped her hips and eased himself into her as they kissed, and she moaned into his mouth when he began moving inside her.

Where their bodies met, he was overcome with sensation. And his breath grew shallow and gasping as they moved in sync with each other. He slid his hands up her sides, toyed with her breasts, brought them to his mouth, took her nipples between his teeth as he teased with his tongue.

He wasn't expecting it when she came so fast. Before he'd even gotten used to having her on top of him, she began crying out, gasping as her body bucked against the orgasm.

He'd been trying to restrain himself a little, move slowly, make sure she had time to come, but she was apparently as pent up as he was, and when she recovered, he kissed her silent and began moving faster inside her.

Harder, faster, until his own orgasm was nearly upon him. He was coiled tight, ready to burst forth, when she came a second time.

Her cries, and the pulsing of her inner muscles against him, were the final nudge he needed for his own release, and he joined her in the gasping, quaking aftermath.

As she collapsed on top of him, he wrapped his arms around her and kissed her gently on the cheek. Spent, exhausted, the last thought he had before drifting off to sleep was that he loved Soleil Freeman. He loved her, and she was about to have his child.

There really wasn't anything else to know, as far as he could see.

SOLEIL EASED HERSELF out of bed, cursing silently with each step she took toward the bathroom. Pregnancy sex might have had the lovely benefit of easy multiple orgasms, but it also brought with it a new set of problems, like how to avoid her lover ever seeing her ass when she had to get up and go to the bathroom.

Once inside, with the door closed, she washed up, put on her robe, then stared at herself in the mirror, trying to see what West saw.

All she saw were the same chipmunk cheeks and wary green eyes that greeted her every day lately. Her hair was sticking up in the back where it had gotten knocked free of a braid while they'd been rolling around in bed, so she smoothed it down and tucked it back where it belonged.

Still no clue about West and his obstinate insistence that she was different than all the other someones out there he might fall for.

He looked at her in a way that made her wholly uncomfortable. He looked at her as if he adored her. And how could she live up to such feelings? They'd only lead to heartbreak. She had to make it clear, once again, even though they'd had sex—even though it was hot and wonderful and all that—that they still faced the same issue of her not wanting him the way he wanted her.

She was a wretch. They'd made love, and all she could think of was how to stem the flow of good feelings? How about basking in the afterglow for a little while?

Soleil switched off the bathroom light, then eased the door open, peeking out to see if West was still asleep. She could see down the hallway and into the bedroom, where he still lay on the bed, his eyes closed.

She went back and lay down on the bed next to him, on her side, but before she could get up close and pretend to be asleep herself, he rolled over and looked at her.

"Hey," he said with a sleepy smile.

"Sorry, I didn't mean to wake you."

Something about getting up close to him, within the range of his power over her, made her forget whatever it was she'd been so bent out of shape about in the bathroom. It was probably pheromones or something. He pulled her to him, and she sighed a happy little sigh as she let herself be enveloped in his warmth.

She'd chill out with him for a bit, allow herself the simple comfort of a hot guy on a cold day.

"What's with the robe?" he said. "I barely got to enjoy the view."

She rolled her eyes.

"You really do look beautiful pregnant," he said.

Before she could stop him, he'd undone the belt of her robe and pushed it aside, revealing her right side, breast, belly and legs.

"Yeah, yeah. I'm not into the whole round, bulgy look."

"You should be. Our baby's in there. Growing inside your body. That's pretty damn amazing. What's not beautiful about it?"

He had her there. She didn't know what to say. Anything that came to mind would make her sound like a shallow dolt, and really, he was right.

She may not have exactly welcomed the changes to her body, mostly because they were strange and unexpected and didn't fit with her image of herself as a strong, capable woman who could bend over and reach her toes with ease.

She hated to think that she'd bought into even the slightest bit of beauty-industry brainwashing that told her she was supposed to hate herself unless she was a size two with flawless skin and smooth hair. But maybe she had let such ideas seep into her consciousness. This was America, after all—it was impossible not to harbor a few unhealthy notions about beauty.

During her brooding silence, West had started stroking his hand over her belly. "Have you felt her kick lately?"

"It's more of a fluttering feeling than a kick. Not anything you'd be able to feel yet. But in a few more months, I hear she'll be using my ribs for soccer practice."

"I don't want to miss that," he said, his expression turning tense.

"Yeah. You'll be in Colorado again… How much longer until your assignment there is up?"

"Anytime now. I'm waiting to get orders for an overseas assignment."

Soleil's entire being recoiled at the idea of West going to some dangerous unknown location. Surely it was just her pacifist upbringing. She didn't want to see anyone go off to a war-torn country, and especially not the father of her baby. But… This wasn't the usual sense of dread she got—this was stronger.

He noticed her reaction. "It's terrible timing, I know. For this," he said, nodding at her belly, "and for the situation with my dad. I'm not sure what to do."

"Right." Her voice, flat, to match the look in her eyes, probably.

"I know what you're thinking. Why would I want you to pick up your life and move with me when I won't even be around half the time?"

"I didn't say that." But, yeah, she was thinking it.

"I don't have any good answer. I only know other military families make it work because they believe in serving their country."

"You might note that I'm not exactly a duty, honor, country kind of girl."

"I know. But some things are more important than our preconceived notions of what we will and won't do, or what kind of community we fit in, aren't they?"

Typical West, trying to bully her into seeing his point of view, rather than accepting that they disagreed.

Exactly why she didn't want to have him in her life 24/7.

She tugged her robe back down to hide her exposed body and pulled it tight against her chest.

"I'm doing it again, aren't I?" he said before she could compose a proper comeback.

"Doing what?"

"Trying to bully you into seeing things my way. I told myself I have to stop that, but… Old habits." He smiled weakly. "I'm trying."

Not much she could argue with there. He knew what he was doing to annoy the hell out of her, and he was trying to change it. Maybe they'd be able to work well as coparents, at least, even if long-distance.

"I appreciate that," she said.

A sound from the front door caught her attention, and Soleil sat up, her ears straining to hear if it had been a key in the lock that she'd heard.

"Hello? Soleil? I'm home."

"Oh, God," she whispered. "It's my mom."

"We finally get to meet?" His wry smile suggested he was enjoying her discomfort a little too much.

"No! Not now!" She stood and hurried to shut the bedroom door. Before closing it, she called, "Hi, Mom. I'll be down in a minute."

"Why not?"

"Because she's crazy, and I'm not ready for it. I'll never hear the end of it from her, once she has specific details about you to grill me with."

"She's going to have to meet me sooner or later."

He stayed on the bed, naked, looking as though he was in no hurry to get dressed.

Soleil stopped in the middle of tugging on her panties and jeans. "Fine, you want to meet her? Get dressed and come right downstairs. You'll see."

He chuckled. Taking his sweet time, he eased himself up and started gathering his clothes. Soleil put her bra and sweatshirt back on, smoothed her hair and began straightening the duvet to hide the evidence of their midday sex.

"Maybe I should take a shower first. Get cleaned up so I don't smell all musky when I meet your mom."

"Just hurry up. She's going to eat you alive, either way."

West pulled on his jeans and took the rest of his clothes with him to the bathroom, while Soleil went downstairs.

She found her mother in the kitchen, unloading a paper bag full of groceries—all meat and vegetables, of course.

"Weren't you a vegetarian before you went on this cleansing diet?"

Anne turned and gave her a look from head to toe. "Smells like you've been—"

Yikes.

"Painting?"

Whew.

"Yeah, putting a second coat of paint on the baby's room. It's still not finished."

"You shouldn't have chosen such a dark color. Aren't nurseries supposed to be pastel?"

"Yes, and if I were painting the room pink or lavender," Soleil said in her sweetest voice, "you'd criticize me for gender stereotyping the baby."

"Yellow is a good nursery color. I've always loved the effect of yellow on walls."

Soleil turned on the kettle and started making tea. It was damp and cold outside, and the dreary weather was seeping into the house, into the room and into her mood all of a sudden. And her mother was not helping matters.

"Next time you paint a nursery, you can make it as yellow as you want," she said as she tried not to clench her teeth.

"What's that sound upstairs? Is someone taking a shower?"

"Yes, someone is taking a shower." Soleil slammed the sugar container on the counter a little too hard, and the lid slipped off and clattered onto the counter.

From upstairs, she could hear the water shutting off. She had three minutes max before West would be down here getting tortured by the great Anne Bishop.

Her mother finished putting away the groceries and began to assemble a salad. She eyed the sugar Soleil was about to put in her tea.

"Do you know how bad for you refined white sugar is? And for your baby?"

"It's pure evil, I know."

"Are you going to tell me who's upstairs, or shall I wait to be surprised?"

"It's West, the guy who knocked me up," she said, knowing how much her mother hated that phrase and relishing the sound of it as it tripped off her tongue.

Knocked me up.

So satisfying to say, and so perfectly crude, so base in its imagery. It was the perfect phrase to infuriate a feminist poet.

Though, for West's sake, she probably shouldn't have been trying so hard to get under her mother's skin.

"Oh? So you two are still fooling around. I thought you weren't a couple."

"You know how us postfeminist girls are, always having sex without commitment. It's exactly what your generation envisioned, isn't it?"

"My generation did not ever envision intelligent women like yourself getting *knocked up,* as you put it. And we never expected those younger than us to be so entirely crude and disrespectful of all we worked for."

"You were working so hard for the feminist cause when you cheated on Dad, weren't you? It was all about sexual liberation and had nothing to do with your own fragile ego, did it?"

She hadn't planned to say it, but now it was out there, hanging in the air between them like a rotten odor.

Her mother spun, pinning her with a dark look as she pointed a knife at her, ever the drama queen. "I will not stand here and be abused," she said, her voice barely steady.

"Is telling the truth abuse?"

"The history of my personal life is my own business."

"Oh? Does that mean my personal life is my own business, too?"

"Why are you so hostile?"

How like her mother to change the subject when the argument wasn't going her way.

"I'm not answering any questions while you have a knife pointed at me."

"And I'm not staying here if you're going to abuse me." She slammed the knife down on the counter.

"I thought you enjoyed pain. Or is that just what you claim in your writing because it sounds good?"

"Hello, ladies." It was West, standing in the kitchen doorway.

He must have overheard part of their conversation, because he looked as if he was about to jump into shark-infested waters.

"Captain West Morgan, meet my mother, Anne Bishop," Soleil said.

"Captain?"

"Yes, Mom. West is an air force officer," she said,

lapsing into her chirpy fifties housewife voice again. "He bombs innocent civilians for a living."

Her mother's expression neutral, she looked from Soleil to West. "How nice," she said. "If you'll excuse me, I'll be leaving now. If you care to stop acting like a monster, you can reach me via my cell phone. I'm going to find a vacation rental for the rest of my time here."

"You don't want to stay here? But why?" Soleil, blinking innocently, hadn't managed to infuse her voice with anything resembling sincerity.

Her mother began packing up her groceries again, furiously flinging heads of lettuce and sides of meat into her shopping bag.

West watched the whole scene, bewildered. Probably not sure if he should be offended at her description of his profession or relieved that he wasn't in the line of fire at the moment.

Without planning to, Soleil had rescued him from her mother, she realized. And, she understood, too, she actually wanted to be the villain in her mother's eyes, for reasons she didn't quite understand.

"Ms. Bishop, I hope you're not leaving on account of me," West said, stepping into the room now, his voice sounding confident. "I remember reading your poetry in college. It's an honor to meet you."

He'd read her angry feminist poetry…at the air force academy?

Soleil didn't believe him for a second, but she

kept quiet. She took the kettle off the stove before it started whistling and poured the hot water into a cup with a lemon-ginger tea bag.

Her mother could never quite hide her pleasure at being recognized as a renowned poet. She smiled stiffly. "Why, thank you for saying that. I'm sorry you've walked in on Soleil and me at our worst."

"The scene's not much different at my father's house, between me and him. I think it's the holidays—this time of year makes everyone tense."

Her mother's posture changed a bit, went a little less stiff.

"Would anyone else like a cup of tea?" Soleil asked.

No one seemed to hear her. Anne was staring at West now as if she was seeing him for the first time.

"I've always said the holidays are the most miserable time of year. All the pressure to be happy and normal, to make everything perfect. It's unnatural, isn't it?"

"Absolutely," West said.

"I'm going to leave you two lovebirds alone. I'll be packing," she said, sounding a lot less tense.

"You don't have to leave, Mom."

"This is one less way we have to pretend everything's perfect, okay? We'll both be a little saner if we have a bit of space."

Her mother left the room, and Soleil felt stung that suddenly she was the only one being childish. At the same time, she owed West. He'd saved her and himself.

She mouthed the words *thank you*. He grinned back at her.

"I'll have a cup of that tea," he said. "Oh, and before I forget, my mom asked me to invite you and your mother to her Christmas party this coming Saturday night."

"That's sweet of her."

"It's from six to whenever. No gifts or anything—just show up. She lives at the Redwood Shores condominium complex on the north side of the lake. She's in unit seven."

"I think I can remember that."

"I was thinking, um, I'd like to come by the farm some more, you know, to help out around here."

"That's not really necessary. I've got the routine down, for the most part."

Except she hated getting up early and at this time of year tended to be slack about farm upkeep.

"How about cutting yourself a break? You run this place on your own, you're almost six months pregnant and you've got an eager farmhand willing to help out for free."

He had a point there.

"Okay, if you really want to help out…"

"I'll come by in the morning then," he said, probably trying to seal the deal before she changed her mind.

As she'd feared, she was being railroaded, but for some reason she wasn't able to muster up the will to protest.

CHAPTER FOURTEEN

JULIA HAD TAKEN to avoiding her computer entirely. After her first date with Frank, she'd lost the nerve to respond to his calls or e-mails. She felt terrible about it, but she'd feel even worse if she were going on dates and falling in love while her ex-husband sat with mashed potatoes crusted on his face and no one allowed near to tell him he needed to wipe his mouth.

These were the kind of humiliating issues he faced on a day-to-day basis now. A once-great man—albeit an impossible one—reduced to childhood problems.

Okay, maybe she was crazy. Or maybe she was a coward. But Frank surely couldn't have been as perfect as he seemed. She was simply saving herself the trouble of a big letdown later.

She was too old for romance anyway. That was a notion best reserved for the young and foolish.

But still… She felt terrible when she thought of Frank.

So, she stayed away from her computer and cringed when she checked her voice mail.

It was Julia's night off from General duty while

West stayed with his father. She was hosting her annual Christmas party in four more days, and some people would be RSVPing via e-mail, so she had to go online.

This year, she was in no mood to host, but it was a party she always threw, and people looked forward to it. She couldn't let them down. Being with John again put her in a terrible mood, frankly. She could hardly stand herself the past few days.

She reluctantly sat at her desk and started scanning her in-box for responses, studiously trying not to look at the couple of messages from Frank Fiorelli, which she hadn't even opened yet.

But curiosity finally got to her, and she clicked on the most recent one.

Dear Julia,
I'm sorry I haven't heard from you. Regardless of whatever changed your mind about seeing me again, I want you to know I think you're a lovely person. It was my pleasure to meet you, and I wish you a life filled with love and joy.
Yours,
Frank

Shame washed over her. She'd never ignored a letter in her life, and it nearly killed her to do so now. What was she to say? *Oh, sorry, but I've been too busy taking care of my ex-husband to go on a date with you.*

Nothing made sense, and it all seemed like proof that she was too old to date. At her age, women were caring for their aging husbands, not having coffee-shop meet-ups with their online-dating buddies.

Have a nice life, Frank Fiorelli, she thought. *I'm sorry I won't be a part of it.*

WEST CLOSED the gate on the goats, who were staring at him warily with their strange eyes through the four-rail fence. He bent to give Silas a rub, and the dog seemed to smile at him.

He'd shown up at the crack of dawn to get the animals taken care of because he wanted to do it then leave, to make the point to Soleil that he wasn't coming around to see her, that he really, genuinely wanted to help.

Okay, maybe there was something a little dishonest there. Because he did want to see her. But this was their baby's future he was fighting for. He had to do whatever it took to make sure Soleil accepted him as more than some "coparent" who saw his kid on holidays and vacations.

He'd never imagined himself to be the kind of guy who'd enjoy agricultural work, or living on a farm, but he found himself wanting to be here far more than he wanted to be at his mother's or father's house right now. That probably had more to do with the people in each location than anything else.

And the physical labor allowed him to focus all his energy on something besides brooding over his problems.

Being here gave him a glimpse of a life he might have lived, had he had different parents, a different upbringing and different career aspirations.

He crossed the lawn to the house and stopped on the porch to remove his work boots. Soleil was inside doing something in the kitchen, he could see through the window, and he wanted to say a quick hello before heading to his father's house.

Also, he'd made an appointment for a tour at a nearby nursing home tomorrow, and he wasn't sure he could go there alone. Since his mother would never forgive him for even considering the place, he couldn't ask her to go.

He knocked, and after a few seconds Soleil opened the door.

"Wow, thank you so much," she said. "You didn't have to get here to do chores so early."

"It's really nice here at dawn, with the mist hanging over the hills. I enjoyed it."

She smiled. "Yeah, it *is* beautiful."

Another thing he loved about Soleil—how passionate she was about her farm. It was hard to imagine her living anywhere else. Which certainly made a strong point in favor of her never wanting to join him in a military life.

"Would you like to have some breakfast?"

"Thanks, I'd love to, but I have to get back to my dad."

"Maybe next time."

"I was hoping you might do me a favor," he said.

"Um, sure. What is it?"

"I'm supposed to tour a nursing home tomorrow, and—"

"I'll go with you," she said solemnly.

"Thanks. I'll be here early to tend the animals, and then we'll leave around ten?"

"Sure."

West wanted to come up with more to talk about, to stay, linger over breakfast, take her upstairs and make love to her the way he had the day before. He'd hardly been able to sleep last night, he'd been so tormented by memories of her body.

Being with her felt like where he belonged, and the farther he was away from her, the more unsettled he seemed to feel.

But he needed to be at to his dad's house. His mother was under more strain than she'd been willing to admit, and he didn't like leaving her alone with his father for long.

"Well," he said, ending their awkward silence. "I'd better get going."

They said their goodbyes, and he left. Once at his dad's, he found his mother looking even more tense than she had the day before.

She was in the front yard, her shirt stained with what looked like orange juice, attempting to wind up the garden hose.

"What's going on?"

"After your father flung his juice at me over breakfast, he came out here and claimed he needed to wash the car. All he did was spray the cat with the hose."

"Where is he now?"

"Inside, listening to the damn radio again."

Damn? His mother had said *damn?* She never used profanity.

Ever.

"Mom, why don't you take a break and let me handle this for a while."

"I'm fine," she said, sounding anything but.

"Why did he throw his drink at you?"

"Because I told him we're divorced."

West sighed. "Do you think it's a good thing that you're here, and he thinks you're still his wife?"

"What can it hurt?"

"You, for one."

"I said I'm fine. Now leave it alone, West."

He took a step back, reeling at her tone. He felt five years old again, being chastised for breaking the Tiffany lamp that she'd inherited from her grandmother.

"Mom, tell me the truth. Why are you putting up with all this?"

West started helping her wind up the garden hose,

but she stopped and looked at him, her expression grimmer than ever.

"You'll understand someday, when you look back over your life and see that you've been married to someone most of your adult years."

"You're not married to him anymore."

She sighed and took the wound up hose from him, then carried it to the edge of the house and hung it where it belonged. When she returned, she placed a hand on his arm. "This must be confusing for you, me here with your father."

"This isn't about me."

But maybe it was, a little bit. He couldn't deny that it felt weird, having his mother and father together again.

"You're right, it isn't, and I hope you'll understand that I feel I need to help your father."

"He's getting worse, Mom. Can't you see that?"

She frowned, and he knew she'd seen it, too. "I can't let your father be cared for by strangers," she said, her voice growing unsteady. "And if you were the kind of man your father and I raised you to be, you wouldn't, either."

His mother rarely lost her temper, and she insulted people even less frequently. Her words stung him like a slap.

Before he could respond, she turned on her heel and marched into the house.

He stared after her, weighing his options. In the

end, he went inside because he had to make sure his
father wasn't hurling things at her or hitting her. And
really, he didn't have anywhere else to go.

THE NEXT DAY, West was relieved to get away from
his parents' weird dynamic and set off to the farm
again. He went about the morning chores with even
more relish than usual, and when he was done, he
had breakfast with Soleil. Then the two of them
rode together to the nursing home on the far edge
of Promise.

"Are your siblings willing to help at all with
your dad's care?" Soleil asked as they passed the
sign for the home.

"Both of my brothers are refusing to deal with the
situation. They think things are okay as they are,
with Dad chasing away his caregivers. And now
that Mom has stepped in, I don't see how I can
convince them that they should be anything but
complacent."

"Does your mom like to being the martyr?"

West had never thought of it that way. There
wasn't any other way to explain her actions now.
Loyalty should only go so far.

He turned the car into the nursing home parking
lot and found a spot near the door. No, not a nursing
home, the sign on the front of the building reminded
him. A residential-care facility. Could they make it
any more sterile sounding?

He sighed. "This is supposed to be the best place in the area," he said, sounding even less enthusiastic than he felt.

"I did an internship that involved visiting nursing homes while I was working toward my master's in social work. I know a few things to look for, to see if they're a good facility, I mean."

West sighed, his stomach twisting up at the thought of putting his dad in this place.

This was not a fitting setting for the last years of a great man's life, or at least it didn't look like it judging by the squat stucco structure. The building seemed nice enough, spread out before them like a ranch house on steroids. The lawn and trees were carefully groomed, dotted with benches where residents could sit and enjoy the scenery. Except no one was outdoors, and everything was eerily still, as if death hovered nearby, waiting to claim its next victim.

"Come on," Soleil said, placing a hand on his thigh to shake him out of his stupor. "We're here. We may as well get out of the car and see what it's like in there."

West blinked, looked down at her hand, then up at her. She gave him an encouraging smile.

"If we sit here much longer," she said, "we're the ones who're going to be spending our golden years here, not your dad."

He was suddenly overcome with gratitude that she'd agreed to come with him. It had been a long time since he'd had someone in his life he could rely on in tough times, and he'd never felt about one of those people how he felt about Soleil, the woman who was carrying his child.

Okay, this wasn't exactly the time to let his thoughts go off in that direction.

He got out. When they entered the building, a scent of air freshener mingled with urine and cafeteria food assaulted them, and West had to force himself not to turn and walk out the door. To the right was a reception desk, where a blond woman had her head bent over some work, and to the left was a lobby and sitting area, where a television squawked, its volume up a little too high, to accommodate the hard of hearing, presumably.

Elderly residents in various phases of immobility were scattered about, arranged either facing the TV or facing the large picture window that looked out on the parking lot. A few people, not in wheelchairs, had clearly gotten to the lobby by their own means or with the assistance of walkers. These would be his dad's peers.

West approached the reception desk, but Soleil spoke for him.

"Hi," she said. "We're here to take a tour of the facility."

West looked around as she continued talking to the receptionist. His gaze landed on a man sitting with his back to the rest of the people in the room. He was the only person not looking at the TV or out the window. Instead, he was staring somewhat vacantly at West, as if he recognized him but couldn't quite place him.

"Hi," West said, taking a few tentative steps closer. "Do I know you?"

"You're Michael," the man said. "My great-grandson, right?"

This man was probably twenty years older than West's father, at least. In fact, most of the people here looked ancient compared to the General. It was some kind of cruel joke that his mind was failing him so early, while his body was still relatively strong and healthy.

West sat next to the man. He still had a bit of something white and crusty on his lower lip and chin, probably from breakfast, and up close, he smelled as if he could use a bath.

"How do you like living here?" West asked, ignoring the case of mistaken identity.

"In this shithole?" the man said. "When are you going to get me out of here?"

West wasn't quite sure how to answer that one.

"You know," the man continued. "They steal my stuff. My gold watch disappeared last week, and a couple of months ago my wedding ring vanished from my nightstand. How do you like that? First you take away my house, and my car, and you put me in this goddamn prison—"

"Mr. Doran," a nurse said, approaching from the hallway. "Is there a problem?"

"This is my great-grandson," he answered, introducing West.

"Actually, I'm not related to him. I'm afraid it's a case of mistaken identity."

"Oh? Are you my tour?"

West nodded. "West Morgan," he said, standing and extending his hand to the nurse.

She shook his hand, looking puzzled. "Susan Lieberman. I'm the assistant director here. Didn't you bring your father for the tour?"

"That would not go over well. He's suffering from Alzheimer's and is generally resistant to anything new."

Susan nodded sympathetically. "Say no more. It can be difficult helping a resistant family member transition to a new living situation, especially when dementia is involved."

A new living situation was about as euphemistic a way as she could have said it. Transitioning to life in prison without parole would have been more accurate.

Soleil, who'd disappeared into the restroom next to the reception desk, returned. She searched West's gaze to see how he was doing, and he felt instantly comforted that she was there, looking out for him. It was kind of ridiculous how much one little look from her could bolster him.

"Shall we get started?" Susan said.

She and Soleil introduced themselves, but when it was time to follow Susan down the hallway, he couldn't make his feet move. He looked over at the man next to him, Mr. Doran, the nurse had called him, and he tried to imagine his father sitting there instead.

No, he couldn't.

He shook his head.

Soleil caught his eye, her expression growing more concerned. "Are you okay?" she asked quietly.

"I have to get out of here."

She frowned and placed a hand on his arm. "I'm sorry," she said to the nurse. "We're going to have to come back another time."

West didn't hear what the woman said next because Soleil was escorting him out the door, into the cool air that thankfully smelled nothing like urine or cafeteria food.

She guided him to a bench, where he sat gratefully.

"You looked like you were about to pass out in there."

"I—I can't put my dad in that place."

"Are you sure? It may not seem ideal, but trying to care for him on your own might be more difficult than you can imagine right now."

"I'm sure."

They sat in silence, staring across the empty lawn, as the people inside were probably staring at them.

"Thank you," West finally said.

"For what?"

"For being here, for dragging me out of there, for keeping your head when I lost my cool."

"That's what friends are for," she said.

Friends. Not lovers, but friends. Any other time, he might have taken offense and pouted at the distinction, but right now he understood that Soleil *was* a friend. If that's what she wanted to call herself, it was fine by him.

CHAPTER FIFTEEN

THE DAY OF HIS MOTHER'S Christmas party, West was stuck alone with his dad all day. His two brothers had arrived in town, but they were busy visiting friends and had predictably bowed out of Dad Duty.

"Where's Julia? Why isn't she here? She'd know where the book is."

His father glared at the bookshelf, intent on finding a title he couldn't remember. He pulled a book down, grunted in frustration, then put it back. On and on this went, as West looked over the work file he'd brought along with him.

A folder containing a review he needed to write of one of his subordinate officers sat open on his lap. He hadn't had time to get to it yet, it was due as soon as he got back, and he couldn't force his brain to focus on it. Instead, he could only dwell on the fact that he wasn't fit to write reviews of other officers, when his own personal life was so screwed.

Since when did officers go around having illegitimate babies to unwed mothers? Okay, sure, he sounded old-fashioned, like his father, but it was true.

He didn't know a single officer who'd experienced a situation like his. He was surrounded in his work life by married couples and families, and those who were single aspired to be like the ones who'd already paired off—or at least they purported to.

His father dropped a book, then muttered a curse as he bent to pick it up.

This study haunted West. He'd always thought of himself having such a place of his own someday, just like his dad. But now… This wasn't anything like he'd imagined. Sitting here now, reality seemed to mock his small fantasies.

"Dad?" West said.

No answer.

"I'm going to be having a baby soon."

Assured his father wasn't really listening, and oddly comforted by the act of talking to no one in particular, he continued, telling him all about Soleil's pregnancy again, since he surely didn't remember hearing about it the first time around.

"She's the most beautiful woman I've ever known," he said. "And she doesn't want to move to Colorado. She wants to stay here, and I can't. I'm going back to Colorado Springs after the holidays, and I guess I'll be one of those long-distance dads who only sees his kids on holidays.

"It won't be so different from being deployed, like you were a lot—"

"Don't be a fool."

West was startled out of his daze. He looked over at his dad, who was staring at him with a look of utter disgust on his face. His eyes had lost the air of confusion that seemed to be there lately, replaced by the old fierceness.

"What?"

"You heard me. I said don't be a fool. You think your career is going to keep you warm at night? You think your career is going to take care of you when you get old? Look at me and your mother. Where would I be today if it wasn't for that woman? She's the best thing that's ever happened to me, and there's not a day that passes by that I don't know it's true."

West blinked in confusion. Then his brain caught up to his father's time warp. He might have been more coherent than usual, but he was still convinced he and Julia had never gotten divorced, apparently.

West hadn't ever felt sad about his parents' divorce. He'd been old enough when it happened to see that it was the best thing for his mom, and that his father had had it coming. But now…now he felt the loss of what his father thought he still had.

"If there's a good woman about to have your baby, and she won't come to you, you'd better come to her, you damn fool. Do whatever you have to do. Get down on your knees and beg if you have to, but don't pass up the chance to have a wife and a family. It's all that matters."

His father shook his head and shuffled out of the

room, done with the conversation apparently, leaving West to contemplate yet another way he'd managed to disappoint his father.

Only this time, it was particularly ironic, because here he was, putting the military first, the way his father had always done. He'd learned well from the old man.

He'd learned everything he knew about how to be a man from him, and he was well on his way to making all the mistakes his father had made.

God, it was true. He'd become his father, in spite of everything. Here he was feeling as if he'd been the rebellious child, the disappointing one, and he'd been completely blinded to the fact that he was doing everything he could to fill his father's shoes.

Shoes he hadn't thought he'd wanted to fill.

"Julia!" His father was calling as he wandered down the hallway. "Julia! Where are you?"

West closed his eyes. When did the easy part begin? When did he start feeling like the grown-up who knew what to do, and not the child trying to hide the broken lamp behind his back?

Except, he did know what to do.

All he needed was the courage to do it.

As Soleil stood near the entrance to Julia's kitchen, she tugged at the front of her black velvet dress. It was made of a stretchy fabric that allowed her to wear it even though it wasn't a maternity dress, but the downside, she realized now, was that it kept sliding up her belly, creating a completely unattractive effect with the front hemline of the dress too high and fabric bunched up on top of her belly.

She surveyed the crowd, counting faces she knew, though she realized after a moment, she was looking for West. He'd said he needed to watch over his father and bring him, and she'd tried not to put too much weight on the fact that they were starting to act a tiny bit like a real couple…and she was starting to miss him when he wasn't around.

Her mother was at the bar, pouring herself a stiff drink. They'd ridden to the party together in an awkward silence, punctuated by her mother's occasional attempts at humor—comments such as "Aren't we the happy little family?"—followed by her put-upon sighs when Soleil gave no response.

Soleil felt bad now, though, because she saw, once she had a few inches' more space to consider it, that her mother had been trying to make peace as best she could. In a less well behaved state, she would have spent the entire car ride spewing vitriol.

"Soleil!"

She turned to find Julia standing beside her. "Hi," she said. "Your place looks so nice. I love the decorations." She indicated the glimmering tree and the garland hanging from the ceiling.

"Oh, I have to do something to keep myself busy in my old age," Julia said in her usual self-deprecating way.

"You do enough work for ten people."

Julia waved away the compliment. "I never really learned to sit still, is all. By the way, have you seen West?"

"Not yet."

"This is the first time I've invited my ex-husband to the Christmas party," Julia said, leaning in close and lowering her voice.

"Maybe we can put him in a room with my mother and let them entertain each other."

"I'm so glad your mother could make it. She's such an interesting lady."

"And you're such a diplomat, putting it like that." Soleil gave a wry smile and took a sip of the alcohol-free punch she'd poured herself a few minutes earlier.

As if she sensed she was being talked about, Anne turned from the bar and headed right toward them.

"Julia," she said when she reached them. "Thank you for inviting us."

She held a whiskey on the rocks in one hand, and a carrot stick in the other.

"It's so good to see you again. I'd like to introduce you to another friend who's a poet, soon as he gets here. I think you'll like him."

Her mother nodded and smiled faintly. She was wary of other writers, who tended to either feel intimidated by her accomplishments or else want her to read their work and pass it on to her agent.

"That would be lovely," she said without sounding as if she meant it.

Julia was gracious enough to ignore her mother's tone. "If you'll excuse me, I need to check on some cream puffs in the kitchen."

Soleil took another sip of her drink and eyed the tableful of finger foods nearby. She hated this kind of stand-around-and-chitchat party, but who didn't? Everyone in the room looked at least as awkward as she felt, so she vowed to get over herself and make the best of it.

Anne's holiday attire consisted of a gray cable-knit cashmere sweater of the sort women of a certain income level wore, and a pair of cream-colored dress pants that were exquisitely cut. This was her new, gussied-up mother, apparently, since she'd left her house in Berkeley and moved to ridiculously tasteful Mill Valley. Some part of Soleil found it offensive that her once-braless tie-dye-wearing mama, the one who'd railed against the establishment and shacked up with a Black Panther, was now all polish and cashmere.

When exactly had that happened?

Some time, apparently, during all the years they'd grown more and more distant.

And Anne was right that it had been Soleil's doing. Here she was now, taking offense even to her mother's overly tasteful choice of sweaters.

She needed to suck up her bad attitude and get a little Christmas spirit.

"Are you sure you wouldn't like a real drink?" her mother asked, eyeing the glass of punch as if worms were crawling out of it.

"Mom, pregnant women aren't supposed to drink."

"Right, that's what they're telling us, isn't it? Another way to keep the little women nice and quiet and dull, isn't it?"

"This isn't a feminist issue, it's a medical one. Fetal alcohol syndrome is real."

"In my day, a woman could have a cocktail without getting a guilt trip over it, and the babies came out fine."

Soleil could feel her blood pressure rising. "Right, Mom. Of course."

"Look at you! I had at least two glasses of wine a day up until the day you were born."

She wasn't going to get into an argument here, not at Julia's holiday party, so she said nothing. Arguing would only make her angry and make her mother more combative.

So she turned her back and walked away. Across the room, she saw a friend from town whom she wanted to say hi to, but before she could reach her, the front door opened and West walked in, followed by a smaller, thinner version of the man Soleil knew was the General.

"Oh, good, you're here," she said, smiling with relief. "You can save me from my mother."

West looked grim as he shrugged off his black wool coat. "You remember my dad, don't you?"

He did an introduction for the benefit of his father's bad memory, and John Morgan scowled at Soleil as he muttered a greeting.

"It's good to see you, Mr. Morgan. How are you feeling?"

"Somebody's damn cat keeps getting in my house. I'm gonna get my gun and shoot the thing if it doesn't stay the hell away."

"Dad, you're not going to shoot the cat." West gave Soleil a look.

"I have a farm, you know, Mr. Morgan. We could always use a cat there, if you'd like me to take him," she said.

Two rescued cats already lived in the barn, but she could accommodate another one, surely.

"Could you really?" West asked, looking relieved.

"Of course."

Thank you, he mouthed as his father began fumbling with the buttons on his coat. "Never seen the varmint before in my life, and it wanders in through my front door like it owns the place."

He was on the verge of pulling off a button.

"Dad, let me help you with that." West made a move to take over the unbuttoning, but his father swatted his hands away a little too aggressively.

"I can take my own damn coat off! I'm not an invalid."

Julia, as if sensing the discord, arrived at West's side.

"Oh, good, you're here!" she said, giving him a hug.

"John, I could use your help in the kitchen, if you'd like," she said to her ex-husband.

West and Soleil exchanged a look over Julia's head.

"Are you sure about that, Mom?" West asked her, but she ignored him and took the General by the arm, leading him away.

West let out a sigh of relief. "You should have seen me trying to get my dad to leave the house. He insisted he had to stay home and watch some television show that hasn't been on the air in twenty years."

"How'd you get him to come with you?"

"I told him Mom was waiting for him." West shook his head. "Whatever weird time warp Dad's caught in, it's one where he's still married to Mom. Only this time around, he seems to do what she tells him to do more often than not."

"Wow, so maybe it really is a good thing she's offering to help you with him?"

West shook his head, his expression grim.

But before he could explain, someone cried out, "Look who's here—the two lovebirds."

Soleil turned to see her assistant, Michelle, smiling at them. They hugged, and Soleil whispered to her, "Stop looking so smug."

Michelle whispered back, "How can I? You two are adorable."

Soleil flashed her an evil look, which Michelle carefully ignored.

She hugged West next.

"I'm so glad you're sticking around for the holidays this year," Michelle said to Soleil. "I don't think I've gotten to see you for Christmas as long as I've known you."

Soleil nodded. "Yeah, I guess this is the first time I've stayed around, isn't it?"

"You'll have to come over for my New Year's Eve party! It's going to be great—we're getting a Slip 'n Slide for the front yard."

"Won't it be too cold for that?"

"Not if you drink enough. I mean, not you, exactly, but the rest of us. No pregnant chicks allowed on the Slip 'n Slide."

Soleil liked to think of herself as mature enough not to worry about things like being left out of the New Year's debauchery, but she was beginning to feel as if she couldn't breathe for some reason.

There was something about having West here, people assuming they were a couple, and all that... How had her life stopped resembling her own so fast?

Her mother approached their group, an evil gleam in her eye. Or maybe it was the whiskey she'd been drinking. Either way, it meant trouble, and Soleil's entire body tensed.

"Mom, you remember my friend Michelle, don't you?" Soleil said, hoping to distract her.

"Of course. You're the one married to the playwright, aren't you?"

224 BABY UNDER THE MISTLETOE

Michelle nodded. "I left him home with a cold tonight, poor guy."

"Good for you. I've never understood why women are so willing to be the nursemaid."

"It sort of goes with the territory."

"Exactly!" her mother exclaimed a little too enthusiastically.

Soleil cringed. "Mom…"

"Which is why these two should not get married. Don't you think they've got the perfect situation here, Michelle?"

Her friend blinked, stunned at Anne's words. "Um, I guess that's up to them, isn't it?"

"Marriage isn't a relationship of equals—it's a power struggle."

"How would you know when you've never been officially married?" Soleil asked as evenly as she could. "And why are you even talking about marriage?"

"I'm trying to head off disaster at the pass. You get knocked up, next thing you know everyone's peering at your finger, looking for a wedding ring. Believe me, I know. I lived it."

"That was thirty-five years ago. A few things have changed since then if you haven't noticed."

"We pay lip service, but nothing's really changed. You'll see."

"I personally love the power struggle," Michelle jumped in, trying her best to lighten the mood. "It's *great* for our sex life. Especially when I'm the one winning," she said, grinning big.

Soleil could have kissed her friend. She'd effectively shut her mother up. Her mother, the big avantgarde poet, was remarkably uncomfortable with public discussions of sex.

Public discussions that involved humiliating her daughter—no problem.

But sex? Definitely a problem.

Soleil gave West a look, silently thanking him for putting up with her mother. His eyes were smiling, even though he was trying his best to keep his expression neutral.

He was on her team.

"You look like you could use a little fresh air," he said, leaning in close. "Why don't we step outside on the front porch for a bit? Or maybe go for a walk?"

"That would be great," she said, letting him guide her toward the door.

Once they were outside in the cool night air, Soleil took a deep breath and exhaled, watching her breath form a steamy cloud.

"Wow, ten minutes here and the fireworks show has already started," West said.

"Ugh. My mother—"

"She is who she is. No changing her now, right?"

"She gets worse with age."

"Maybe we should water down the whiskey bottle before she has another drink."

"That's a brilliant idea," Soleil said, laughing. "Except she keeps a flask in her purse, too."

God, it felt good to laugh. And once she started, she couldn't stop. She laughed until her belly shook and tears streamed from her eyes.

West, a little bewildered by her outburst, grinned nervously as he waited for her to recover.

"She really does get to you, doesn't she?" he said once she'd nearly calmed down.

"It's either laugh or cry. Or both," she said, wiping the dampness from the corners of her eyes.

West looked up at the night sky, where it was remarkably clear. Stars glittered from above, even more visible than usual.

After a few silent moments, he turned back to her. "Are you warm enough to go for a short walk?"

"Sure," she said, thrilled at the idea of getting away from the tension in the party.

They walked for a bit in silence, admiring the twinkling lights on the houses nearby, and the glow of the moonlight on the lake beyond the homes. Once they reached the lakeside, they walked along the path that circled this part of Promise Lake.

"Have you ever heard how Promise Lake got its name?" West asked, breaking the silence.

"No, actually. I haven't."

"One of the men who settled this area had a bride he left back East when he came here for the gold rush. He was apparently madly in love with her, and he wrote her a letter promising when she came out to live with him, he had a whole beautiful lake that would be hers. He was going to build her a big house at the edge of it, and they'd be rich and live happily ever after."

"That's quite the fairy tale," Soleil said, but she was in more of a mood than usual to buy such nonsense.

"Anyway, his bride was killed on the trip out, and he was heartbroken. The story goes that he never did marry anyone else, simply lived out his life alone here, in a little shack."

"So how'd the lake come to be named Promise?"

"Well, he did strike it rich enough to own all this land and name the area whatever he wanted, but he never did build the big house. He called it Promise because looking at the lake always reminded him of the promise he wasn't able to keep."

Soleil laughed, but okay, she was a tiny bit touched by the story. Not much, though.

West took her hand and stopped her. She turned to face him.

"I know you're not much on romantic notions, but I hope you'll tolerate me getting a little sentimental now."

Maybe it was the cold, but Soleil's eyes began to sting, and she had to blink a lot to keep them from watering. "Okay." she said.

"I'm in love with you, Soleil."

She hadn't been expecting it. She'd been enjoying the walk. But here it was, the thing she dreaded.

"I'm glad we're going to be having a baby together."

"I am, too," she said weakly.

"I want us to get married and be a family. Will you marry me?"

She felt her throat close up. She didn't want it to end like this.

"Come with me to Colorado and wherever else I have to go. We can hire someone else to run the farm until I'm eligible for retirement. Then we'll move here and run it together. It'll work—we can make it work."

"West," she said, feeling horribly sad and tired all of a sudden. "I can't," she said. "I just can't."

"You're not even going to think about it?"

"You know how I feel."

"But—"

"I'm sorry," she said, turning away, heading back toward his mother's.

And she was. But now she saw through all the romantic notions, that he really hadn't changed at all, and they really weren't meant to be.

CHAPTER SIXTEEN

SOLEIL PEERED at the of purple paint, trying to decide if the wall needed a fourth coat. Was it her imagination, or was there still the faintest bit of white showing through?

She couldn't know because she'd been staring at the nursery walls so long, she was nearly cross-eyed.

The sound of the doorbell jarred her out of her puzzlement, and she muttered a curse as she put the paint roller in the pan and headed downstairs.

If it was her mother again, she was going to scream.

But when she opened the door, she found Julia, holding a huge gift basket full of baby things.

"Hi," Soleil said. "What are you—"

"I'm sorry to drop by like this. I talked to West, and he told me about you two…and I felt so bad. This didn't seem like a conversation to have over the phone."

"It's okay, come in," Soleil said, her stomach knotting at the mention of West and what he must have told his mother.

That she was evil. That she'd broken his heart.

That she'd ruined their baby's chance to have a nuclear family because she was too much of a selfish, feminist, career-obsessed shrew.

"This is for you." Julia handed Soleil the basket after she closed the door.

"You really shouldn't have. Thank you."

"I couldn't resist. Now that we know it's a girl—Oh, Lord, the cute baby-girl stuff out there!"

Soleil smiled. "This is so generous of you. I was just painting the nursery. Would you like to see it?"

"I'd love to."

Soleil led her up the stairs. When they reached the nursery, she set the basket inside the crib and turned back to Julia.

"So this is it."

"The color is beautiful. It's like being inside a jewel."

"It's really peaceful, isn't it? I thought with all the light this room gets, it could handle a dark color."

"And this crib!"

"West and I picked it out."

Julia put a hand over her mouth as she admired the mahogany woodwork. Then her expression turned pained as she looked back to Soleil.

"I want you to know that you're family—we're family. Whatever has happened between you and West, I know it's not my business."

Soleil nodded. "Thank you for saying that."

"It's hard raising a baby on your own. I never really had to do it, but I did endure a lot of long deployments being a military wife—sometimes a year at a time—so I know how lonely it can be, and I want to be here for you."

"That's very kind of you—"

"I'm not just saying it, Soleil. I'm very serious. I want to be a big part of the baby's life, if you'll allow me to be."

"Of course I will. You'll be her grandmother."

Crazy, crazy, crazy, how life twisted and turned. A year ago, Julia was simply a kindly older woman in Soleil's book group. Now she was someone Soleil would depend upon greatly.

Julia was studying her, looking thoughtful. "I'm not sure if you know this about West, but he tries more than anyone else I know to do the right thing."

"That's an admirable trait," Soleil said evenly, not wanting to get into a discussion of West with his own mother.

Not now, especially.

"I know this is awkward, and I'm not trying to defend him for whatever he's done to keep the two of you apart, but do keep in mind that his heart is in the best possible place."

Tears pricked Soleil's eyes unexpectedly. She nodded, unable to speak without her voice cracking.

Julia gave her a hug and a reassuring pat on the back, and Soleil was grateful for the moment to recover.

Why she was feeling so emotional now, she couldn't say. Maybe it was hormones, or the impending holidays, or the sadness of knowing she wasn't going to be able to give her baby the nuclear-family ideal that, for a moment or two, she'd allowed herself to believe might really happen.

Maybe it was more about what she'd secretly longed for as a child, rather than whatever her own child might or might not desire.

"How about a cup of tea?" she finally said, her tone light in a way she hoped didn't sound too forced.

"I'd love that."

The two women went to the kitchen, and Soleil put on the kettle.

"Is chamomile okay?"

"Perfect," Julia said as she walked around the kitchen, smiling at what she saw. "This is such a beautiful, cozy place you have."

"Oh, thanks, I haven't changed it much. It's mostly how my grandparents had it, minus the frumpy curtains and stained recliner chair."

She laughed, shaking her head. "What is it with men and those recliners?"

"I'm surprised my grandfather didn't take his to the grave with him."

"Of course not. That would have kept future generations from enjoying it," Julia said, laughing, as she sat at the kitchen table.

"How's it going at your ex-husband's house? I mean, your taking care of him—is it working out okay?"

"It's…sort of working. I got into an argument

about it with West the other day. He doesn't want me to be there."

"Must be hard seeing your ex-husband in the state he's in."

"It is hard. I don't think West understands how hard it really is for me, or why I feel responsible for taking care of John now."

"Why do you?"

She smiled in such a way that it looked as if she was about to frown, and she shook her head. "Because, for a big part of my life, I expected to. Some wedding vows are harder to break than others."

"Do you ever want to remarry, or have another partner?" Soleil asked, curious about Julia's real life, the one she didn't reveal to her son. There had to be more to the woman than the perfect facade suggested.

"Perhaps, if the right person came along."

The kettle began to whistle. Soleil retrieved it and poured them each a cup of tea, then returned to the table with the cups.

Julia fiddled with the tea-bag string, looking as though she had something to say, but for a while saying nothing. Then, finally, "Can I tell you a rather embarrassing secret?"

"Of course, if you want to." If Soleil wasn't mistaken, she'd swear Julia was blushing now.

"Have you ever seen those online-dating sites? The ones with the pictures and personality descriptions and all that?"

"Sure, who hasn't?"

"I met a man through one of those sites."

"Julia! That's great. Who is he?" The whole idea of West's mom online dating was so incongruous with Soleil's image of her, she could hardly wrap her mind around it.

"His name is Frank, and he's retired, working as an artist now. He owns a little gallery in Guerneville, too."

"Is that where he lives?"

Julia nodded.

Soleil leaned forward, placing her elbows on the table, smiling to indicate she wanted every juicy detail.

"And? Are you two dating? In love? What?"

"No, none of that. The truth is… We e-mailed, and we talked on the phone, and we met a couple of times and I really liked him, but…"

"You lost your nerve?"

She nodded.

"I think it's so brave of you to try something new, put yourself out there. My own mom has just given up on ever having a relationship again because she's too disillusioned. But look at you—online dating. That's the best thing I've heard in a long time."

"Oh, it's completely ridiculous. Someone my age creating a dating profile. It's humiliating is what it is." She was shaking her head, staring at her cup of tea as if she couldn't even bear to meet Soleil's eyes.

"No, no, no. You've got it all wrong. You're apply-ing old-fashioned notions about dating to the contemporary world, and the truth is, everything's changed. None of those old rules apply."

Julia looked doubtful. "You're very sweet to say that, but…"

"How did you leave things with Frank?"

"I've ignored all his e-mails and phone calls since our first date."

"Why don't you call him and explain you had a case of nerves but that now you're ready to see him again?"

She shook her head. "It's not that simple. I…when I heard about John being sick, and needing someone to take care of him…"

"You felt guilty for having fun?"

"I couldn't let myself be with Frank. It's hard to explain. I guess, when I was with John, I always imagined us taking care of each other in our old age…."

"It's incredibly generous of you to help the way you have," Soleil said, but something shifted inside her. Some essential piece of her well-being had gotten knocked out of place by Julia's comment, and she felt suddenly uncomfortable.

"Sometimes, I don't know if I'm being generous or stupid."

She forced herself to set aside her own discomfort and focus on Julia's problem.

"John is lucky to have you in his life, but you shouldn't stop living your own life in order to help him, you know."

Soleil took a sip of her tea and savored the almost-sweet taste of the chamomile, as the aroma itself had an instant calming effect.

"It was too much to take in all at once—John's illness, the stress of dating someone new. I suppose I'm getting to be a bit of an old dog who—"

"Oh, stop it! You're one of the most vibrant, active people I know. You accomplish more than ten people on most days. It was perfectly normal for you to freak out over a first date, though. When's the last time you dated someone?"

Julia flashed a self-deprecating smile, then winced. "I haven't really dated in, maybe, eight years. I saw a man briefly, a few years after my divorce, until things fizzled out, but other than that, no one."

"No wonder you're scared. You haven't been on the dating scene since your early twenties, and you introduce yourself to it with online dating? How did that happen?"

"I accidentally clicked on one of those darned pop-up ads while trying to make it go away."

Soleil couldn't help it. She laughed out loud.

"Well, good for you," she said.

Julia rolled her eyes. "And I went and blew it my first time out. Frank must hate me."

"I doubt it. If he's a decent guy, he knows how hard it is to find a woman like you. I bet he'd be thrilled to hear from you again."

"You really think so?"

Soleil placed her hand on top of Julia's on the table, and said, dead serious, "Do me a favor? Call that man and apologize. Make a date with him, okay?"

The older woman looked doubtful, but she finally said, "I do owe him an apology. Maybe if he's open to it—"

"He will be."

"But what man is going to understand that I have to be my ex-husband's full-time caregiver?"

She squeezed Julia's hand then. "You don't have to be. In fact, I don't think you should be. I think it's going to eat you alive emotionally." Soleil normally tried not to be so meddlesome, but this one time, she felt as though she needed to speak the truth.

"Someday you'll understand—"

"I *do* understand, and I'm not saying you shouldn't be there for him at all. I only mean, the job you're taking on is too big for any one person to handle. You need to step aside and let your sons be responsible for providing their dad's primary care."

Julia shook her head. "They've all got their own lives, and they're all so busy—"

"They'll figure it out. You giving up your life isn't the right solution. Maybe they'll find a trustworthy male caregiver who John won't be able to bully so easily. And you could visit a few times a week if you want, or lend a hand here and there, but really, Julia—"

"Now isn't the time for me to play the martyr, is it?"

Soleil shook her head, relieved her message was being heard and not dismissed.

"Thank you," Julia said quietly, sliding her hand out from under Soleil's and giving it a soft pat. "I came here to offer you help, and you helped me instead."

"It was nothing. I'm always happy to talk over tea."

"I've got an appointment, so I'd better get going, but I'm so glad we talked," Julia said, standing up.

Soleil followed her to the door, each step closer to being alone again reminding her of the way she'd felt a few minutes ago, when Julia was talking about caring for her husband in old age.

They said their goodbyes, and Soleil closed the door, watching through the window as Julia went to the car and drove away.

Now the house was completely silent, save for the sound of the ticking antique clock in the living room.

Tick, tick, tick…

Julia's absence left a gaping hole that was sucking Soleil toward everything she didn't want to feel.

She walked upstairs to the baby's room, hoping to distract herself with one final coat of paint. Physical activity would make her feel better, keep her mind off negative thoughts….

In the purple room with the empty crib and the basket of baby gifts, she was sure she'd feel soothed. This was the safe haven she was creating for her baby. This would be the scene of countless happy hours in her future.

Just her and the baby.

Together.

Alone.

They'd have each other, but...

She recalled what Julia had said, about ties that couldn't be undone, and the ache within her grew more and more unbearable until she couldn't help but cry.

She sat in the middle of the hardwood floor, put her face in her hands and cried for what she didn't have.

A partner, a lover, a father, a friend.

A family.

Sure, she and her baby would make a family, and they would love each other. But it would be lonely the same way her own childhood had been lonely, and someday she'd be bitter and alone, the way her mother was bitter and alone.

Yes, she was on the road to becoming her mother, when what she really wanted was to be more like Julia, warm and open and loving.

She was exactly like her mother, whom she couldn't even share a house with, without having a major fight.

Was she dooming her poor baby girl to the same fate, by not being able to break out of her mother's mold?

She was crying so hard drool formed a long ribbon from her lower lip to the top of her pregnant belly, and she felt more pathetic than she ever had in her life.

She was alone, feeling sorry for herself, and utterly pathetic.

All she needed now was a whiskey bottle and a penchant for angry poetry, and she could change her name to Anne Bishop Junior.

CHAPTER SEVENTEEN

JULIA DELETED everything she'd just written. Nothing sounded right.

The main problem was, this wasn't a matter she should have been handling via e-mail. And the other problem was, she was terrified to call Frank Fiorelli again.

She tried again.

Dear Frank,
I'm so sorry to have ignored your calls and e-mail. I had a family emergency, and—

No, too stilted.

She ought to pick up the phone and call. Or maybe go to see him.

But it was the day before Christmas Eve, and she didn't know his address. She knew where his studio was, but would he be there today?

She had to try. If he wasn't there, at least she could leave a handwritten note to tell him she'd stopped by, which was better than an impersonal e-mail. Yes, that's what she'd do.

Julia jumped up from her desk chair. If she hurried, she could make it to Guerneville by four o'clock. Then maybe, if Frank wasn't at his studio, she'd call him and let him know she was in town, see if he wanted to meet for a drink.

Her stomach knotted as she hurried to the bathroom to check herself in the mirror.

Same silver-blond bob as always, same brown eyes. She added a bit of lipstick, and her face instantly brightened. Then she grabbed her coat and headed out the door.

An hour later, she was parked in front of Frank's gallery. A light was on in the upstairs studio, she could see from the street, and her hour-long case of butterflies became twice as intense.

During the whole car ride, she'd told herself he wasn't going to be there, and yet…

The light was on.

The gallery was open, and she could see through the window that Frank's daughter was busy helping a customer. A handful of other customers milled about the space, creating a welcome diversion for Julia to walk in and go straight up to the studio without having to explain her rudeness.

She made it through the gallery without being spotted, and she climbed the stairs to the sound of someone hammering in the room above.

When she reached the landing, she saw Frank wearing a pair of work goggles, poised over a table, nailing one piece of wood to another.

"Hello?" she called.

Frank looked up, clearly surprised at the interruption.

When his gaze landed on her, she expected to see annoyance, maybe even anger, but all she saw was confusion, and then… A tentative smile.

"Julia? What a surprise. What brings you here?"

She could feel herself blush. "I owe you an apology," she said.

He put down the hammer, took off his goggles and rounded the table.

Julia took a tentative step forward, and Frank closed the distance between them.

"What happened?" he said, not unkindly. "I was worried you'd decided I was a pervert or an ax murderer."

"Oh, no!" she said, appalled all the more. "It wasn't you at all."

"Then what? I was really hoping to see you again. I'm glad you're here, in fact." He smiled gently, and Julia got her first inkling that everything really was going to be okay.

"I was hoping I could explain everything over dinner," she said. "My treat."

Frank's expression transformed into a frown, and her stomach twisted up. Oh, dear. She'd been too forward.

"Call me old-fashioned," he said, "but I never have gotten used to a lady paying for dinner. At least not the first few times around. But we can work that out later. I know a nice little Italian place around the corner."

She breathed a sigh of relief. "I hope I'm not interrupting your work."

He waved a hand toward the table dismissively. "You're rescuing me from another evening of utter frustration," he said. "I haven't done a single good thing since you disappeared on me. Typical self-centered artist—I nearly managed to convince myself you vanished because you hated my art so much."

He laughed, and Julia melted.

"I love your work," she insisted. "It's actually a little early for dinner. Would you like to have a drink first?"

"Absolutely," he said, but before she could turn and head for the stairs, he took her hand in his.

He clasped it between both his hands, and he gave her one of those smiles that started in his eyes. "I'm so glad you're here," he said.

Julia smiled back. "Me, too."

SOLEIL HADN'T WANTED to spend Christmas Eve alone. But when the invitations had come from friends, and even Julia, to have dinner with them, she couldn't bring herself to say yes, either.

She didn't have the energy to go out and face people and pretend everything was okay when it wasn't. And her mother had made plans with old friends for the evening.

So Soleil would stay home, maybe watch a movie or read a book, and contemplate her last Christmas without a child. From now on, the holiday would be a big production, and she tried to tell herself she was savoring the freedom to do nothing this one last Christmas Eve.

She had just turned on the Christmas-tree lights when she heard a vehicle coming up the driveway. Past the tree, she could see West's car in the distance, and the tiny knot of dread that had been growing inside her all day transformed in that instant into something that felt like hope.

No, not hope.

Joy.

No, not joy.

Love.

It didn't matter why he was coming now—to deliver a gift for the baby or tell her he was leaving or berate her for being a fool for not being willing to move to Colorado. There was one thing she had to tell him, consequences be damned.

She ran to the door and left it open as she bounced across the porch and down the gravel road toward the car. He stopped when she neared, stuck his head out the window and peered at her, looking confused.

"Is everything okay?" he asked.

"Yes," she said. "I mean, no, everything's not okay."

He turned off the car and got out, staring at her belly as if it might hold some answer.

She took him by the shoulders and looked into his eyes. "I love you, West."

"What?"

She'd never seen him look so stunned—and she'd had some pretty stunning news lately.

"I. Love. You."

"Does that mean—"

"No, it doesn't mean I'll come to Colorado."

"That's not what I was going to say."

"I love you, and I don't know what to do about it. I can't ask you to give up your career any more than I can give up my life here."

He smiled, still looking a little stunned, a little confused.

"You could move here," she said. "Help me run the farm. I could expand the program if I had you helping. We could help take care of your father if you were here."

He laughed. "You just took the words out of my mouth."

"Marry me," she said.

"That's supposed to be my line," he answered, taking a small black velvet box from his pocket. "And this belonged to my mother."

He opened the box, revealing a gold ring.

"Is that a yes?" she asked, her voice nearly catching in her throat.

Could this really be happening? Had he just said he'd move here?

"Of course it is. You're the only woman I ever want to love. Aside from our daughter, of course."

"But…the Air Force. What will you do?"

"It doesn't matter. I'll retire early. My life is here now, with you and the baby. Ever since I saw that ultrasound, there's been a little voice in the back of my head whispering to me what I need to do."

Soleil looked down the winding gravel road that led away from the farm, and that had brought West back to her—that had brought him home.

"You belong here, too," she said. "Just like I do."

"Yeah, I think I do."

And when he kissed her, she knew without a doubt it was true. He belonged here.

With her, loving her, for life.

EPILOGUE

"YOU'RE SUPPOSED to smile, not cry."

Soleil looked up at the camera pointed at her. "Would you put that thing away?"

"No, I want a few more shots. I've heard newborn babies' faces change every day. We have to get lots of pictures or we'll forget what she looked like."

"Oh, God," she muttered, but he could tell she was kind of enjoying the attention.

He clicked a few more shots at various angles, unable to stop himself. They looked beautiful together, Soleil and their little girl.

She smiled at the baby who'd been attached like a suction cup to her breast all morning. "Enough already," she said to the baby, right before she gently pried her off.

"Your turn," she said. "My arms are cramping up."

He put down the camera and took the baby from her.

"Think of any names you like yet?"

"I know for sure that we're not naming her Matilda."

"Mattie for short! I think it's perfect," West said as

COMING NEXT MONTH

Available January 12, 2010

#1608 AN UNLIKELY SETUP • Margaret Watson
Going Back
Maddie swore she'd never return to Otter's Tail...except she *has* to, to sell the
pub bequeathed her, and pay off her debt. Over his dead body, Quinn Murphy tells
her. Sigh. If only the sexy ex-cop *would* roll over and play dead.

#1609 HER SURPRISE HERO • Abby Gaines
Those Merritt Girls
They say the cure for a nervous breakdown is a dose of small-town justice. But
peaceful quiet is not what temp judge Cynthia Merritt gets when the townspeople of
Stonewall Hollow—led by single-dad rancher Ethan Granger—overrule her!

#1610 SKYLAR'S OUTLAW • Linda Warren
The Belles of Texas
Skylar Belle doesn't want Cooper Yates around her daughter. She knows about
her ranch foreman's prison record—and treats him like the outlaw he is. Yet when
Skylar's child is in danger, she discovers Cooper is the only man she can trust.

#1611 PERFECT PARTNERS? • C.J. Carmichael
The Fox & Fisher Detective Agency
Disillusioned with police work, Lindsay Fox left the NYPD to start her own
detective agency. Now business is so good, she needs to hire another investigator.
Unfortunately, the only qualified applicant is the one man she can't work with—
her ex-partner, Nathan Fisher.

#1612 THE FATHER FOR HER SON • Cindi Myers
Suddenly a Parent
Last time Marlee Britton saw Troy Denton, they were planning their wedding. Then
he vanished, leaving her abandoned and pregnant. Now he's returned...and he
wants to see his son. Letting Troy back in her life might be the hardest thing she's
done.

#1613 FALLING FOR THE TEACHER • Tracy Kelleher
When was Ben Brown last in a classroom? Now his son has enrolled them in a
course, so he's giving it his all, encouraged by their instructor, Katarina Zemanova.
Love and trust don't come easily, but the lessons yield top marks, especially when
they include falling for her!

HSRCNMBPA1209

New Year, New Man!

For the perfect New Year's punch,
blend the following:

- One woman determined to find her inner vixen
- A notorious—and notoriously hot!—playboy
- A provocative New Year's Eve bash
- An impulsive kiss that leads to a night of
  explosive passion!

When the clock hits midnight Claire Daniels
kisses the guy standing closest to her, but
the kiss doesn't end after the bells stop ringing....

Look for

Moonstruck

by *USA TODAY* bestselling author

JULIE KENNER

Available January

red-hot reads

REQUEST YOUR FREE BOOKS!

2 FREE NOVELS PLUS 2 FREE GIFTS!

HARLEQUIN®

Super Romance®

Exciting, emotional, unexpected!

YES! Please send me 2 FREE Harlequin® Superromance® novels and my 2 FREE gifts (gifts are worth about $10). After receiving them, if I don't wish to receive any more books, I can return the shipping statement marked "cancel." If I don't cancel, I will receive 6 brand-new novels every month and be billed just $4.69 per book in the U.S. or $5.24 per book in Canada. That's a savings of close to 15% off the cover price! It's quite a bargain! Shipping and handling is just 50¢ per book*. I understand that accepting the 2 free books and gifts places me under no obligation to buy anything. I can always return a shipment and cancel at any time. Even if I never buy another book from Harlequin, the two free books and gifts are mine to keep forever.

135 HDN EYLG   336 HDN EYLS

Name	(PLEASE PRINT)	
Address		Apt. #
City	State/Prov.	Zip/Postal Code

Signature (if under 18, a parent or guardian must sign)

Mail to the **Harlequin Reader Service:**
IN U.S.A.: P.O. Box 1867, Buffalo, NY 14240-1867
IN CANADA: P.O. Box 609, Fort Erie, Ontario L2A 5X3

Not valid to current subscribers of Harlequin Superromance books.

**Are you a current subscriber of Harlequin Superromance books
and want to receive the larger-print edition?
Call 1-800-873-8635 today!**

* Terms and prices subject to change without notice. Prices do not include applicable taxes. Sales tax applicable in N.Y. Canadian residents will be charged applicable provincial taxes and GST. Offer not valid in Quebec. This offer is limited to one order per household. All orders subject to approval. Credit or debit balances in a customer's account(s) may be offset by any other outstanding balance owed by or to the customer. Please allow 4 to 6 weeks for delivery. Offer available while quantities last.

Your Privacy: Harlequin is committed to protecting your privacy. Our Privacy Policy is available online at www.eHarlequin.com or upon request from the Reader Service. From time to time we make our lists of customers available to reputable third parties who may have a product or service of interest to you. If you would prefer we not share your name and address, please check here. ☐

HSR09R

Bestselling Harlequin Presents author

Lynne Graham

brings you an exciting new miniseries:

PREGNANT BRIDES

Inexperienced and expecting, they're forced to marry

Collect them all:

DESERT PRINCE, BRIDE OF INNOCENCE

January 2010

RUTHLESS MAGNATE, CONVENIENT WIFE

February 2010

GREEK TYCOON, INEXPERIENCED MISTRESS

March 2010

www.eHarlequin.com

HP12884

'No, thanks.' Elinor forced a smile and mentally willed him not to demean her with some sordid proposition. 'The only man who will ever take *care* of me with my agreement will be my husband. I'm willing to wait for you to come back but I'm not willing to be kept by you. I'm a very independent woman and what I give, I give freely.'

Jasim frowned. 'You make it all sound so serious.'

'What happened between us last night left pure chaos in its wake. Right now, I don't know whether I'm on my head or my heels. I'll stay for a while because I have nowhere else to go in the short term. So maybe it's good that you'll be away for a while.'

Jasim pulled out his wallet to extract a card. 'My private number,' he told her, presenting her with it as though it was a precious gift, which indeed it was. Many women would have done just about anything to gain access to that direct hotline to him, but his staff guarded his privacy with scrupulous care.

Before he could close the wallet, his blood ran cold in his veins. How could he have made such a serious oversight? What if he had got her pregnant? He knew that an unplanned pregnancy would engulf his life like an avalanche, crush his freedom and suffocate him. He barely stilled a shudder at the threat of such an outcome and thought how ironic it was that what his older brother had longed and prayed for to secure the line to the throne should strike Jasim as an absolute disaster....

* * *

What will proud Prince Jasim do if Elinor is expecting his royal baby? Perhaps an arranged marriage is the only solution! But will Elinor agree? Find out in DESERT PRINCE, BRIDE OF INNOCENCE by Lynne Graham [#2884], available from Harlequin Presents® in January 2010.

Copyright © 2010 by Lynne Graham

HPEX0110B

*Bestselling author Lynne Graham is back
with a fabulous new trilogy!*

PREGNANT BRIDES

*Three ordinary girls—naive, but also honest and plucky…
Three fabulously wealthy, impossibly handsome
and very ruthless men…
When opposites attract and passion leads to pregnancy…
it can only mean marriage!
Available next month from Harlequin Presents®:
the first installment*

DESERT PRINCE, BRIDE OF INNOCENCE

* * *

'THIS EVENING I'm flying to New York for two weeks,'
Jasim imparted with a casualness that made her heart sink
like a stone. 'That's why I had you brought here. I own this
apartment and you'll be comfortable here while I'm abroad.'

'I can afford my own accommodation although I may not
need it for long. I'll have another job by the time you
get back—'

Jasim released a slightly harsh laugh. 'There's no need for
you to look for another position. How would I ever see you?
Don't you understand what I'm offering you?'

Elinor stood very still. 'No, I must be incredibly thick
because I haven't quite worked out yet what you're offering
me.…'

His charismatic smile slashed his lean dark visage.
'Naturally, I want to take care of you.…'

HPEX0110A

"I like it, but I think her middle name should be Soleil."

She sighed. "Okay, fine."

There it was. That was their daughter's name. "Perfect."

She said nothing, but he could tell she was pleased.

He watched her walk, tentatively, unsteadily, across the room to the window, and his heart swelled with pride. She was his wife, and this life, with her here in California, running the farm, it was the first time he could look around and see that his choices finally resembled his heart, and not anyone else's.

the baby rooted around on his chest, only to discover that he didn't have anything interesting there.

She began to howl. He gazed at the tiny pink bundle of screaming, angry perfection that had barged into his life and promptly taken charge of his heart a day ago.

"Let's don't be one of those couples whose baby goes around for a month with no name."

"Alice?" he suggested.

"No."

"Amanda?"

"No."

"Drucilla?"

"Now you're making me angry."

West laughed. "You're so cute when you're mad, I can't help myself."

Soleil eased herself off the hospital bed. Her pink flannel pj's were kind of turning West on, but since they had a baby to keep up with and she'd just given birth and all, he figured he'd better keep that fact to himself for now.

Or at least until she was in a better mood.

"How about Juliana," she said. "It sort of combines both our mothers' names."

He looked down at the baby in his arms, who, for the moment, was lying there peacefully.

"Juliana," he said. "Is that your name?"

"Juliana Morgan," she said, trying out the sound of it.